THE CARIBBEAN
SEDITION

MX Publishing

Other books in the CODE NAME DELTA series:

The Quadrille

Red Goliath

One Deadly Souk

The Magdalena Gambit

Killing for Profit

Man on Target

The Impostor

A New Kind of War

King of the Slaughtermen

A Honey Smeared Trap

To Know is to Die

The Circumstantial Hitman

The Poisonous Hand

Dead Dog Won't Bite

THE SECRET FILE OF PATRICK COONAN

THE CARIBBEAN
SEDITION

Oscar Ortiz

MX Publishing

Book #4 in the CODE NAME DELTA series

To my son Alex Francisco,
my dear 'Big Guy'

Must read 🏆

Praise for The Caribbean Sedition

AWARDED 5 STARS

"A high-octane spy thriller that demands attention, delivering relentless action and suspense that will grip you from start to finish."

— **Reedsy.Discovery**

AWARDED 4 STARS

"The Caribbean Sedition, by Oscar Ortiz, delivers an intense Spy thriller experience that keeps readers on the edge of their seats. Tasked with eliminating powerful Russian mobsters operating under the guise of a money-laundering network, Patrick and Jessica go undercover as a newlywed couple. As the mission unfolds, they encounter unexpected betrayals from their own ranks, intense confrontations, and a gripping car chase that culminates in a near-death experience. The story concludes with Patrick receiving unexpected recognition from Colonel Berkowitz, bringing a heartfelt conclusion to the action-packed events. Overall, the ending perfectly complements the adrenaline-fueled journey of the protagonist, providing a satisfying blend of intensity and emotional depth."

— **The Online Book Club**

THE DEADLY SINGLE-MINDEDNESS OF AGENT DELTA

"Many central characters in books, TV programs and films today are burdened with doubt and have difficulty justifying their actions to themselves. Not so Patrick Coonan, otherwise known as Agent

Delta! This protagonist gets on with the job, dispensing with political correctness and emotional baggage as he sweeps the story along before him. He is not always in complete agreement with his superiors, it's true, but what self-respecting hero obeys to the letter, every time?"

— Arthur Hall
Creator of the Sector III Espionage series

OSCAR ORTIZ SHINES BY HIS OWN LIGHT

Like its predecessors, The Caribbean Sedition *is a novel written with great professionalism and in the best style of the classic spy thriller, for which two of its most representative exponents in the 20th century, Ian Fleming and Donald Hamilton, set the guidelines that would later be picked up by an infinite number of others – among whom Ortiz shines by his own light.*

— Ignacio Cárdenas Acuña
The Dean of Cuba's Noir Detective Mystery writers

CHARACTERS THAT SEEM REAL

"The feel of this series takes me back to the adventures I read back in the 70s with many of those books written in the 60s. [And I ate those stories up!]. Mostly I was reminded of the Nick Carter Killmaster series when written by skilled authors like David Hagberg, Martin Cruz Smith, and especially the highly gifted Ralph Hayes. Like Hayes, the Patrick Coonan adventures author, Oscar Ortiz, can keep the action going while still giving us enough backstory of the characters to make them seem real."

— Randall Masteller
Administrator of Spy Guys & Gals

"Disunion by force is treason."

TABLE OF CONTENTS

FOREWORD

(An introduction to The Secret File of Patrick Coonan)

In recent times, the cinematic James Bond has been converted into a "catwalk muscleman" bearing an asphalt face and a propensity for melancholy. To escape from this new "politically correct" version of the character, incapable of being seductive and without any trace of the model developed by Ian Fleming in his novels, there still are few options available. The most obvious one is to review Fleming's books or the films starring Sean Connery and his most popular successors.

Another option is the pulp narrative alternative to 007, currently well-served by the prolific Cuban American writer Oscar Ortiz. This is the series *Code name Delta*, starring Patrick Coonan, a U.S. Rangers' sniper transformed into a clandestine operator for the Quadrille — the sharp counterintelligence unit created by Ret. Special Forces Col. Marlon Berkowitz to safeguard America from all threats. Always with the protracted shadow of the Cold War as the background, which also served as the main setting in the first Bond book written by Fleming.

Ortiz's virtues as a novelist can be well-appreciated in all his Patrick Coonan adventures: a concise, direct prose, halfway between the noir mystery genre and the spy thriller; utmost erudition in the different topics dealt with, where one perceives a thorough work of research and the offering to the reader of varied plots that combine investigation, violent death, sexuality, and an uncomfortable background of moral sordidness.

Josep Ferran Valls
Valencia, Spain - Oct. 2022

DRAMATIS PERSONAE

AHMED (Commander)
Muslim guerrilla leader of Palestinian descent suspected of spear-heading the Islamic Sword, a most fierce group of jihadists who have declared war on the United States.

ALEDO (Margot)
Acting chief of staff for the Quadrille who also oversees CI5's Shared Archives Department. Mrs. Aledo serves as Col. Berkowitz's personal assistant in matters of administration within the CI5 headquarters.

BENSON (Bruce)
Aide-de-camp to Special Agent Samuel Norwood of the FBI's Organized Crime Division. Works as a team with Agent Greenwald.

BERKOWITZ (Marlon)
A.k.a. the Colonel. A retired U.S. Special Forces colonel, veteran of the Vietnam War and the invasion of Grenada. Founder and director of operations of the Quadrille, currently in command of CI5. Col. Berkowitz is Pat and Jessica's immediate chief.

BRONSOSKI (Nikolai)
Russian banker stationed on the island of Aruba, works with Krakov and Ismailova in maintaining the Ostrovsky clan's money-laundering operation.

BULL (Jackson)
Also known as Jack Bull, he is an agent of the National Reconnaissance Office, currently assigned to track down and capture black-market dealers of Weapons of Mass Destruction.

COONAN (Patrick)
Pat is the best eliminator under Col. Marlon Berkowitz's command: he is, also, one of his most loyal followers among the original Quadrille members and one he completely trusts. His code name is Delta, and he is the protagonist of the series.

FELDMAN (Arnold)
General Director of the Organized Crime Force (OCF). Man of intrigue and great influence in Washington political circles.

FITTS (Jessica)
Intelligence analyst hired by the Colonel to join the new Quadrille, now operating as CI5. She is also Pat's new partner. Her code name is Phi.

GORIAINOV (Mikhail)
Chief of security of the Ostrovsky's clan in Aruba. His duty is to protect the entire money-laundering network known as "the Caribbean umbrella." He works in collaboration with Tiger Kuzekh.

GREENWALD (Len)
Aide-de-camp to Special Agent Samuel Norwood of the FBI's Organized Crime Division. He teams up with Agent Benson.

ISMAILOVA (Emil)
Russian banker stationed on the island of Aruba, works with Krakov and Bronsoski in maintaining the money laundering network.

JOHNSON (Bill)
Alias the Armorer. A senior member of the Quadrille now working as the official armorer for CI5. Also heads the Special Effects section of the unit.

KAILA
Member of an elite team of contract operatives, named Triple K, the Colonel employs to support Pat and Jessica in Operation Parasol.

KARINA
Leader of the elite Triple K Group.

KARMEN
The third member of the Triple K Group.

KODINA (Andrei)

Former chief-of-staff of the Atomic Fang Division of the defunct KGB during the Soviet era and former supervisor of Yuri Pavenko when he was a still a member of the KGB. Kodina is the current president of ROSONOVO-RONEXPORT, the Russian Federation's military equipment export agency under Vladimir Putin.

KRAKOV (Vyacheslav)

Russian banker stationed on the island of Aruba in charge of supervising the money laundering network of the Ostrovsky clan.

KUZEKH (Piotr)

Alias Tiger. A Russian mafia enforcer escaped from a Miami-Dade County prison. He shares security duties with Mikhail Goriainov in Aruba.

NORWOOD (Samuel)

A senior FBI agent currently working for the Bureau's Organized Crime Division; he specializes in the Russian Mafia. During the Cold War Norwood worked in Washington, D.C. hunting illegal spies from the former KGB. Works as a team with Greenwald and Benson.

OSTROVSKY (Oleg)

Russian mobster. Head of the feared Ostrovsky clan, which he runs in partnership with his brother Terek.

OSTROVSKY (Terek)

Russian mobster. Head of the feared Ostrovsky clan, which he runs in partnership with his brother Oleg.

PAVENKO (Yuri)

A former Soviet KGB nuclear saboteur turned into a very dangerous dealer of Weapons of Mass Destruction.

TETRIAK (Nina)

A.k.a. Nina the Gunslinger, she is Pavenko's young protégé, also his right hand in the business, his concubine and main enforcer.

TILSON (Alfred)

During the formation of the Quadrille, he was brought in by Col. Berkowitz as his second in the chain of command that ruled his organization. He was Pat's main instructor during the selection training period. His new position in CI5 is that of Liaison Officer between Col. Berkowitz's subsection and Director Feldman. Promoted in recent times to be the OCF's Regional Control Officer for the Caribbean region. Tilson runs a special task force of twelve operators under his command.

Nobody was certain at the time what Parasol really consisted of, not even Jessica and I, though we had been told that it was a huge financial network well set up by the Ostrovsky clan, a shell company they used to launder all the dirty proceeds from all their offshore operations. That was close enough to the truth. What we did not know was that they were not the only ones. Seeing how convenient their money-laundering operation turned out to be, Oleg and Terek (the clan's big bosses) set out to sell their services to all sorts of radical groups and other organizations of dubious provenance to be used for the same purpose —charging a percentage of the total amount of the laundered capital.

The big drug cartels from Mexico and Colombia, the more elusive black-market arms dealers, the modern pirates of The Horn of Africa and other regions of that continent, for instance, and the dangerous secret societies from the Pacific Rim and certain terrorist cells of the Islamic Jihad, all, absolutely all of them, banked there; until Col. Marlon Berkowitz got his orders from Capitol Hill and tried to put a stop to the operation.

So, he ended up sending me and my partner, Jessica, to take care of the problem with the underhanded help of an FBI task force. This measure finally managed to spoil their party. What we did not know then was that, once again, we would be clashing head-on in the field with another clandestine unit of the Organized Crime Force (a.k.a. the OCF).

Hi, folks, my name is Patrick Coonan, but in the trade, I'm known as Agent Delta.

THE CARIBBEAN UMBRELLA

Part One

Chapter 1

DESTINATION: ARUBA

The helicopter that flew us to Aruba belonged to the commercial fleet of the Royal Sky Flying Group, Ltd., a British company operating out of the Netherlands Antilles. In truth, there was little or nothing British about Royal Sky other than its name; it was a secret electronic tracking station manned by the FBI. But since the Federal Bureau of Investigation owed us favors, having occasionally used our personnel for overly dirty missions in a hunting ground off-limits to them, my boss decided to call in on some fat cats from the J. Edgar Hoover Building on Pennsylvania Avenue and have them throw us a line on this operation. The pilot of the chopper was a very tall albino, with white hair, a square chin, pale pink skin, freckles, and the works; his name was Samuel Norwood, and he was a vet of the war that the Bureau had fought in Washington against KGB illegals. He was a somewhat cynical and soft-spoken fellow, yes, but very knowledgeable about his trade. Along the way, he informed us that the island of Aruba was like a gigantic cruise ship for lovers, those opulent Scandinavian liners that many couples choose to launch their honeymoon. Aruba is an island as small as it is beautiful, floating in the Caribbean Sea just off the coast of Venezuela. It's almost nineteen and a half miles long by six miles wide and it belonged to the Netherlands Antilles until 1986, when it gained its independence. Today it has its own Royal Governor, a democratic government and a 21-member elected Parliament.

That's all I know.

The natives are known for being affable. The waiters, for example, serve you with a genuine smile on their lips and English is a popular language there. It would have been possible for us to fly directly to the island from Miami, via a commercial airline, but we had not opted for this route because of the weapons we were lugging. Our presence in Aruba was not exactly a vacation, and the weaponry we were carrying in specially sealed black duffel bags was a perennial reminder of that.

Through the concave Plexiglas panels that walled off the flight deck, a clear blue sky was visible. The helicopter touched down on the runway appointed by the Control Tower at the Queen Beatrix International Airport, located on the southwestern tip of the island. The FBI man waited quietly for us to descend and unload our luggage, then he made the arrangements for refueling and after that he vanished.

Passing through the Customs checkpoint with the weapons was possible because Alfred Tilson, our man in Aruba, was waiting for us there. Five months ago, Director Feldman had transferred him from his original position as Liaison Officer between the OCF Directorate (which is the same as saying he, Feldman) and CI5, promoting Tilson to Regional Control Officer in the entire Caribbean basin and assigning him his own sub-section. Feldman's move was based on sound logic, because Tilson's experience matched the Colonel's and now, with the Russian mobsters knocking down our doors, there was an increasing need for hardened pros in the field, executive directors capable of guiding and supporting the younger generations in their missions — whatever they might be.

Old Al fit that profile perfectly.

In fact, although not as senior as Tilson and the Colonel, I was also qualified for the position myself. My experience in the field and my years as an eliminator with the Quadrille, allowed me to direct and advise — only that aspect of the job has never interested me. Feldman could have assigned me to another post, the Hispanic Caribbean region, for instance, since I am fluent in Spanish and that area is not exempt from Russian Mafia activities. However, he never did it and I know why: a total lack of confidence in yours truly here.

In short, Feldman's move was coherent and most convenient for him, considering the rivalry between the director of the OCF and my chief, Col. Berkowitz. But after the strange attitude Tilson had shown towards me during Operation Scorpion Tail*, to find old Al there, waiting for us instead of my chief, kind of upset me. I tried to hide my displeasure by forcing myself not to think much of it, I had enough to worry about with Pavenko and Nina Tetriak, the Russian bankers in Aruba and the *boyeviks*** in charge of protecting the clan's interests in the island, to add more fuel to the fire....

In just a matter of minutes, Tilson worked his magic and got us a rental: a sports convertible. Once we were in the car, with all our luggage safely locked in the trunk, we lowered the rooftop to allow the coastal air to cool the cabin. While Phi joyfully steered our dashing red Mustang, I kept track of the GPS indications that guided us to our destination.

During the trip I reflected that this was not the ideal car to be associated with a couple of secret agents on a mission, as it attracted a lot of attention. It's only in

Hollywood productions that clandestine operators like us are seen scurrying around in ostentatious Aston-Martins or those incredible Porsches driven by Tom Cruise in his *Mission Impossible* films. I was very surprised that an old pro with Tilson's background would have supplied us with such a flashy vehicle. No experienced field executive would have settled for it. But I consoled myself with the thought that perhaps that was the purpose that prevailed in our case. To give the opposition's watchdogs the impression that neither Jessica nor I had anything to hide and that we had only traveled to Aruba for a great time on our fake honeymoon. Taking this into consideration reassured me — well, not entirely.

"This really is a beautiful location, Pat," commented my partner, interrupting my train of thought. "It's such a pity that we have come on a mission!"

She was right, of course, I reflected grimly; it truly was a shame.

Our destination's address was No. 43 at J. E. Irausquin Boulevard, and it was one of the most opulent time-share condo complexes rising on the oceanfront in the entire Eagle Beach area. The large sign carved on a marble pedestal at the entrance identified it as La Hacienda Beach Resort & Casino. It was a four-story building, designed to look like a horseshoe, that sprawled around a fishing and water sports emporium, an Olympic size swimming pool with an outdoor bar, a European style bistro with outdoor tables and multi-colored parasols. There was also a man-made cataract.

La Hacienda has eight hundred rooms, four luxury restaurants, three taverns, a two-story ice cream parlor, and a salon dedicated to the enhancement of feminine beauty. There were also three outdoor Jacuzzis, a collective Turkish bath, and a fitness club with masseuses as part of the staff.

At the time, the Eagle Beach hotels had attracted the attention of the OCF because of rumors pointing to the area as the latest acquisition by a shady group of Eastern European investors. In the years following the fall of the Soviet Union, the Russian Mafia had managed to establish numerous fronts in the Caribbean region. Their motive in penetrating the world of global finance was to weave a financial network to launder all the money generated in the business dealings of the Ostrovsky clan. It was the largest and most powerful of all the criminal syndicates to emerge from Eastern Europe.

It could not be proved, of course. As I said before, they were only rumors, but the rumors were supported by sightings of some of their men in the area. Specifically, Yuri Pavenko, whose trail — I found out later — an American agent named Jackson Bull had followed to Aruba, after spotting him and losing him again in Miami.

Since the Colonel had convinced Yuri to become our informant, it was always my responsibility to neutralize those who approached him with intentions of taking him out of the game. The main objective of Operation Parasol (according to both, Tilson and Feldman) was the physical elimination of a man named Mikhail Goriainov, the clan's top enforcer in the island. He was supposed to be the most dangerous man the Ostrovsky brothers had in the shire; but not the only one. There was another character as sinister and brutal as Big Mike, Tiger Kuzekh, who had been sentenced to twenty years in a Miami prison for murder but had managed to escape.

To the list of sentences that my boss had given me during the briefing, other names were added that did not belong to the group of hardliners in charge of protecting the operation. These were the administrators of the complicated laundering network themselves: Vyacheslav Krakov, Nikolai Bronsoski, and Emil Ismailova.

As can be seen, we really had our hands full.

Prior to leaving Miami, we'd undergone a slight change of appearance, in case Pavenko had passed on our descriptions to his associates on the island. Jessica had changed the color of her reddish mane by dyeing her hair blonde; she'd also managed to get a bit of a tan; the sun doesn't get on her easily because she has very delicate skin. I also dyed my hair blond and grew a mustache. So, we became Mr. and Mrs. Peter Jensen, a "lovely couple" of Scandinavian tourists.

We were assigned a honeymooners' suite on the second floor, with a wonderful view of the sea. It was very spacious and decorated to please the most discerning of tastes. When we finally arrived, I hung my wardrobe in the closet while Jessica prepared some drinks. She poured Scotch on the rocks for me, and three fingers of Vodka, mixed with orange juice and some ice cubes for herself. Stripping off my blazer, I loosened the knot of my tie and approached her to receive my drink.

"To your health, Carrots," I toasted.

"To yours, as well."

On the balcony I leaned over the railing and let my eyes roam the landscape. From there you could easily take in a lot of Eagle Beach, a peaceful view of extraordinary natural beauty.

"What are our chances of wrapping up the mission quickly, Pat?" my partner asked.

I shrugged. "No idea, Carrots, what's the hurry? I'd like to give us a little time in these parts."

"It's a wonderful place. Look at the ocean... Such limpid waters! It relaxes me to watch the way the waves break on the cliff."

The sun was setting, but there were still a good couple of hours of light left. I felt the impulse to warn her to watch her words, as we had not yet combed the room for hidden mikes, but I restrained myself. Jessica knew as well as I did that the hotel complex was controlled by ex-Soviet KGB people and those guys, they always were, are very conscious about security.

Despite my morbid musings, I moved closer to my fake blonde wife and embraced her. First, we kissed sensually, and she allowed me to hold her splendid derriere in both hands. As on many other occasions, I felt the immense desire to take her to bed replace all my phobias while continuing to kiss her like this, clinging to her buttocks. Finally, Jessica pulled away from me and took me by the hand.

"Come on, partner", she whispered with bated breath that smelled of Vodka. "Let's get to bed."

*Refer to the third volume in the series, entitled *One Deadly Souk*. (*Author's Note*)
**Russian term given to Mafia enforcers who handle "wet affairs" and other related issues. (*Author's Note*)

*C*hapter 2

FISH, BEERS, AND GUNS

The next day we got up early and crossed the traffic circle to head for the water sports center. At the counter we requested to rent a boat with an outboard engine, or a small yacht, whichever one they had available. To round out the charade we also rented a couple of Scuba tanks with regulators and mouthpieces, foot fins and diving masks. We were asked if we needed the services of a nautical guide, but I turned them down flat. I felt confident that I could handle the craft all by myself. We acquired large portable coolers in which to hide our weapons. Two of them held our entire arsenal and so we moved it from our hotel suite to the skiff. We also bought fresh bait and a couple of heavy rods for deep-sea fishing. In the third cooler we tucked in a couple of pounds of Serrano ham, two loaves of French bread, a jar of mayonnaise, one pound and a half of sliced Swiss cheese and three six-packs of Heineken beer. We hoped to be back before dark to visit the Club Florence and its busy restaurant specializing in seafood dishes, since we had been informed that some of our marks frequented that eatery. But if they didn't show up that night nothing would change. We had plenty of time to complete the mission. As the Colonel had pointed out during our preliminary briefing, this job was to be carried out with surgical precision, not in haste.

Eleven o'clock in the morning surprised us sailing in deep waters, with only hungry seagulls and puffy clouds for company. The weather was excellent, and I managed to get the barge a few miles offshore before shutting down the engines and dropping anchor. Jessica passed me a cold beer; I uncapped it and took a sip straight from the bottle.

"Do you think it's wise to try them here?" She asked.

"What, the beers?" I mocked her.

"No, silly!" She burst out, laughing at my quip. "The guns!"

"Of course, it is, Carrots; you don't see anyone around the contours, do you? Anyway, keep your eyes open while I get them."

"Will do."

I unpacked the firearms with extreme care.

"Jesus, Pat, what is *that*!" She shouted when I gently laid them out on the deck. My heart was racing with sheer joy at the sight of *that* magnificent gun. Perhaps it wasn't the most accurate rifle if fired prior to adjusting its sights (hence my intention to test it before work), but it was going to serve me well because I didn't plan to use it at a real far-off distance. This was a Springfield Super Match, the M1A automatic model, with the stock made of hickory wood. It had a premium steel barrel, and the chamber could hold ten of the .308-caliber cartridges. Almost a commercial replica of the U.S. Army's M-14 sniper rifle. It came with Lake City Match cartridges packed with Federal brand powder and Sierra Matchking 168 hollow-point ammo.

"Bill must be nuts to assign that monster to us!" Jessica spat. "Or maybe it was the Colonel's decision... Either way, I'm not touching that thing!"

"Don't worry, Carrots; you won't have to," I told her

flashing a baleful grin. "This, is men's work!"

"Right."

We spent a good bit of time testing and tuning the guns, being careful to separate the sequence of our shots to minimize the commotion. Although we had sound suppressors, these contraptions never quite succeed 100%, and the noise tends to travel farther as it bounces off the liquid element. Our instructions were to remain "deep-sea fishing" until Tilson showed up and made contact, but we had not been told how or when he would do so.

The man arrived in a chopper.

The helicopter flew over our boat several times, before Tilson took a dive from the cockpit; it was a leap of over thirty meters, mind you. Dressed in Scuba attire, he entered the waters standing upright about a hundred meters east of our position. After unloading his only passenger, the chopper pilot executed a one hundred and eighty degree turn and disappeared the same way he'd come.

"Hey, lads!" Shouted Tilson, once he took the regulator mouthpiece out of his mouth, as he climbed into the yacht, dressed in a neoprene-lined wet suit up to mid-thigh, complete with Scuba tanks. "Pretty nice weather, eh." He unhooked the tanks and set them down gently on the deck.

Tilson was an athletic guy, much more so than me. He towered a good three inches above my six-foot frame, with a trapeze artist broad shoulders and a bullfighter's waist and he moved with the ease of a man half his weight. His agility —quite amusing for someone of his age— was a product of keeping himself in top physical condition. The sun of the tropics had tanned his pale skin; he had a luxuriant head of brown curls, dotted with gray hair; his eyes, with slanted eyelids, were a faded grayish blue, as if the color of his orbs had worn out with the years and the disenchantments of life. He had the broken nose of a boxer, and that accentuated his tough guy looks.

Old Al approached me with a jovial expression and held out his right hand.

"God damn it, Delta! It's been a while, hasn't it?"

"Yes, sir! I guess they're keeping you busy now that you're no longer training the new recruits?"

He crushed my hand with his powerful grip.

"Absolutely." He spoke. "This transfer to take over an OCF post in the Caribbean has changed it all for me. You are right about being very busy, but at last someone in Washington has deigned to recognize my worth. I don't know if you've heard by now, but I'm now a sub-section chief and command a team of twelve operatives here on the island. The Russian mobsters are putting up one hell of a fight, Delta, and with those Islamic Sword miscreants on the warpath, all indications are that we'll have a lot more work cut out for us than we bargained for; thanks to God —or the devil."

"Sure," I said, "just like old times." But I couldn't help noticing how he had carefully avoided any mention of our little incident in the previous operation when he'd openly lied to me about what I considered a very touchy subject. Of course, it was an issue we would not discuss in front of Jessica. She didn't need to know. But I could not erase from my mind all that had happened in Colombia*.

I noticed Jessica didn't say a word. She just stood there looking us over.

*Refer to the third volume in the series, titled *One Deadly Souk*. (*Author's Note*)

*C*hapter *3*

THE LEADING VOICE

Minutes later, stepping inside the yacht's cockpit, we took chairs around the coffee table and Tilson stripped off his neoprene jacket. Fastened with adhesive Velcro straps to the side of his torso, he carried an oversized pouch made of waterproof material. He sneezed loudly before detaching the pouch from his skin and set the contents on the table: three flat electronic tablets loaded with information. He passed one to each of us and kept the remaining device for himself.

"It looks like you guys stumbled into a hornet's nest, back in Colombia," he said activating his tablet and motioning us to do the same. "As you will see in these reports, the trail left by Yuri Pavenko points first to Miami and then to Eagle Beach," Tilson said in a very off-hand manner, and I couldn't help but wonder if he was aware of the secret arrangement that Col. Berkowitz had going with the Russian, or just ignored it — but that was *very* unlikely. "Before we go into details, I want to give you an overview of the activities of the Russian Mafia in this region. Open file number three, please."

We did and Tilson continued.

"In little more than a decade after the collapse of the Soviet Union, a total of six hundred billion dollars has been sneaked out of Russia by the KGB and used to make investments in the Caribbean. Stealing and hiding assets from the national treasury is no easy task, and the CIA, always on the lookout for the movements of its former rival, was the first to detect how the KGB set about the task of organizing the small criminal gangs that dominated some of their cities before the fall and providing them with state-of-the-art equipment to collaborate in the laundering process. Almost two thousand shell companies were set up, with accounts in banks of little seriousness... By the way, lads, these reports we have here were all submitted by our Moscow Bureau."

He paused again and Jessica uncapped a cold beer and set it in front of him on the table. Tilson smiled at her and said: "Thanks, Phi, you're one lovely girl."

She gave him a listless smile, but I wasn't too pleased with the exchange because there was an instant, however fleeting, when I seemed to catch her running her eyes over the man's nearly perfect thoracic musculature.

"Tell me something, Al," I spat with every intention of dispelling the captivation those tanned muscles seemed to exert on my partner, "what is it about Russian law enforcement agencies these days? The territorial militias of the former MVD were very competent, why open an OCF division in Moscow to pull their chestnuts out of the fire? I don't understand..."

"On the one hand, it is too complicated to explain," he said, scratching his forehead. "On the other hand, I don't have time for it, nor is it relevant to this case. So, if you don't mind, lad, let's stick to your mission, shall we?"

He ignored the murderous look I threw him and shrugged off my question with a frugal nod.

"At present," Tilson went on, "Russian law enforcement agencies are considered inept or have been penetrated and corrupted. Many prosecutors and officials take bribes; others succumb to threats from gangsters, which is *why*, Agent Delta, an OCF division has been established in Moscow and a police academy in Budapest to better train and monitor new officers emerging from the former Eastern Bloc republics."

Tilson paused, perhaps to raise the spout of the bottle to his lips and take a sip, or maybe to allow the weight of his words to fall on us; well, on me. After all, who was I to doubt whether an OCF branch should be opened or not in Moscow? And it was at that instant that I was overcome by the troubling feeling that behind that calculated pause there was something else... However, all this happened in fractions of a second and then Tilson went on:

"As you know, the OCF is in the process of reforming, and so is the Quadrille. In fact, you see we've stopped being a lone wolf outfit and started operating more closely with all the other branches, although I understand CI5 only has jurisdiction over the Americas while the OCF covers the entire world. The primary objective of the Organized Crime Force remains one: to take down the Russian Mafia. So, whether your unit is called the Quadrille, or CI5, it will need to play by the new rules... I hope, for everybody's sake, you are both clear on that." This last sentence was spoken deliberately while looking straight at me.

"Understood," I sighed.

"Phi, you got a problem with that?"

"No, sir."

"Good! Let's move on then."

Both Phi and I nodded silently.

"The thing is we have a little problem, the arrival of that fella from the NRO has come to complicate matters."

"Who do you mean?"

"A Jackson Bull from the National Reconnaissance Office, ever heard of him?"

"Not really. Why do you ask?"

"That fuckin' lad is a nuisance! This 'Jack Bullshit' guy is after the same prey that has prompted us to get involved in what's going on in Aruba: Yuri Pavenko."

I drew a long breath and repeated the odious name. "Ah, yes, old Yuri... The creature from the Black Lagoon."

"Exactly. The same one you left for dead in New York so many years ago and who later 'died' again in a plane crash in Bogota and whose corpse you identified."

The man was lying, of course. He knew very well that the whole thing was a farce, but since we were in front of Jessica, and, apparently, he was aware that she didn't know the truth, I had no choice but to bite my tongue and curse him to death for laying it thick on me.

"Forgive me, lads," he continued, "but the mess you two caused in Colombia has no precedent. Your orders were to *eliminate* Yuri and his entourage, including that crazy Jihadist commander and the drug baron they called The Scorpion if given the chance, right?"

Phi looked at me with some concern and I held Tilson's gaze briefly without admitting or denying anything at all.

"So, guess what happens... Pavenko and his girl get away unharmed and so does that fuckin' guy, Ahmed, robbing you lads of a briefcase with a quarter million dollars that belongs to Uncle Sam... Taxpayers' money for God's sake! And, to top it all off, Agent Mortimer Long from the Moscow Bureau loses his life in the raid. Now, you tell me if that's not a major fuckup!"

He paused briefly to focus on me. "What kind of work is that, Delta? I've never seen you perform so sloppily.

Nobody's perfect, I know, but there are limits! Do you know how disgruntled Director Feldman is with you? Well, it's not you who's utterly responsible. Neither is she," he said now turning to look at Phi. "But Mr. Feldman wants to fire all of you! Beginning with your chief!"

The most significant of all the rhetoric he employed that morning was this reference to my chief. Certainly, a low blow on his part, but I immediately snapped it off and said to myself that, if things had already reached that point between them, the Colonel would also be aware of it, or should have been, even if he had not shared it with me.

Bite your tongue, Coonan, your turn will come, I thought.

"And now," continued Tilson, softening his tone a bit, "let's study your marks in this operation. I know you were briefed in Miami, but it never hurts to have a good refresher, and besides, I want to see how much you really know to fill in any gaps that might exist in your minds; Operation Parasol is a complex mission, don't kid yourself about it, and the stakes are high, oh yes! Open file number four, if you will. Let's start with you, Phi."

The way he said it gave me a very bad feeling, because I suddenly sensed that his purpose in making us talk was not exactly to correct any apocryphal information we might have had, but to absorb *everything* we knew as if deep down he feared we knew too much.

"Very well," said Jessica and cleared her throat before speaking up. "The entire Caribbean region is dominated by the Ostrovsky clan. They own a legitimate bank in the Bahamas and have bought a hundred citizenships and passports in Dominica. In Antigua, Terek and Oleg Ostrovsky own banks, lending institutions and insurance companies, not to mention multiple investor visas. We also know that they've tried to acquire a bank in Panama but were rejected by the authorities. In the Netherlands Antilles they have controlled access to finance companies and indemnification firms. In Mexico, they lease luxury cars under false names and steal them to ship them over to Russia and other former Soviet republics in the Baltic... Well, am I missing anything?"

I noticed the oft-repeated way the word *bank* kept surfacing on Jessica's little speech and filed this information away in some corner of my mind.

"It doesn't seem so. You've described to the hilt the scenario that is being contemplated in these parts. What about the marks you've have been assigned to eliminate?" Tilson asked, turning to face me this time.

"Target number one: Goriainov, Mikhail. The most dangerous man the brothers are counting on in Aruba." I spurted out. "We didn't have time to delve into his past, but I guess that is your job."

"Of course, I have his file in my possession. Go on."

"Target number two: Kuzekh, Piotr; a.k.a. Tiger Kuzekh. A specialist in contract killings. He has a criminal record in the States, was kept in a Miami-Dade County jail until he managed to escape from confinement. He doesn't qualify as high on the efficiency scale as comrade Goriainov, but he's nipping at his heels.

"Kuzekh is a product of the street, while the other has schooling," clarified Tilson. "However, don't underestimate him, the Tiger can be as witty as his colleague when he puts his mind to it. He is said to be a nutcase, and his bloodlust is matched only by his exaggerated sexual appetite."

"Target number three: Krakov, Vyacheslav. Banker

by profession, at one time he belonged to the USSR diplomatic corps and was also a member of the former Soviet Ministry of Economy."

"Watch out for that one," Jessica interjected. "He may not be an action guy, but he is a force to reckon with. Krakov has a brilliant mind and specializes in global finances. He oversaw an economic delegation in Paris and left Russia when Boris Yeltzin won the first election. Although there are grey areas in his file up to 1994, he is believed to have been one of the best financial advisors the Ostrovskys have. INTERPOL claims that Krakov is a true financial genius and the architect of what is now known as the Caribbean Umbrella."

Therein lay the key to what Tilson was after or should have been: The Caribbean Umbrella.

"Where did you get that one, Phi?" he asked, frowning. "I've never heard of it before!"

"Few people have, sir; but it exists. It's also known by Umbrella-C, *La sombrilla del Caribe*, or just Parasol."

"And?" Pressed Tilson, now most definitely intrigued because it seemed that my partner knew something that he was unaware of —or pretended to be unaware of, to us— and that was no good at all. Not if you are the Regional Control Officer and executive director in the field of a house-cleaning operation as sensitive as this one, get it? Either the man was inept (which I knew old Al never was) or he was playing dumb. Both possibilities worried me.

In any event, my partner Jessica had become the leading voice in our briefing.

"The year 1993 marked a boom time for the Ostrovsky clan, it was when its leaders set out to build empires overseas. The Israeli gangs were very powerful and had also crossed the oceans to begin operating in our continent. On the other hand, the Colombians continued to rule in the field of drug trafficking, and, in addition, they also had to deal with the Mexican cartels. So many competitors seemed to hinder the Ostrovskys' advance. The older members of the clan advocated invading the market Cossack style. Crush the Colombians and drive them out of the arena, kill the Mexicans, liquidate the Israelis, and negotiate with the Italians in New York for the time being and then steal their territory bit by bit. But Vyacheslav Krakov came up with a brilliant idea: Parasol, The Caribbean Umbrella.

"This plan was based on not attacking the competition directly but invading the Caribbean islands with investments until they could establish a well-structured money laundering system, through which they could control their rivals and charge them a percentage for it at the same time. In addition, it allows them to launder their own income at home without taking great risks. Krakov selected two points to start his project; actually, there were three, but the attempt to acquire a bank in Panama backfired. So, he focused on Antigua and Aruba... A large percentage of the money moving through these islands today is clan dough, money that has been extracted from their other operations in Eastern Europe. But at the end of 1994 they suffered a financial setback, and this forced them to set up the Mexican operation, stealing and exporting luxury cars and exotic sports models. In that they have been extremely successful.

"They've also expanded the black-market arms sales with the direct help of Yuri Pavenko, who was the best man they had for that, despite being a somewhat seditious and self-reliant operator. It is believed that it was Pavenko who set up the Devil's Bazaar in Afghanistan and is now trying to do the same here in South America. Of course, Yuri is just the guy for it. His position as a former KGB agent and his friendly ties with the GRU has opened a lot of doors for him; not only to some of the nuclear arsenals of the former Red Army, but also to BIOPREPARAT, that chemical weapons lab secretly operated by the KGB's Directorate XV, with depots in Moscow and in what is now known as Kazakhstan, in Central Asia. Oh, yes, and ROSOBO-RONEXPORT, the military export agency of the new Russian Federation, which, by the way, is run by the infamous *gospodin*** Andrei Kodina... Remember him?"

She paused briefly to stare at Tilson, first, and then at me.

Andrei Kodina? I mused. The name rang a bell, true, but I couldn't place it. However, Tilson did.

"Jesus, are you serious, Phi? Kodina oversees ROSOBO-RONEXPORT?" he inquired while appearing dumbfounded, an incredulous expression distorting his face.

"If he isn't, he's going to be soon, sir, and believe me when I tell you that I share your astonishment; I too cannot explain how the hell a high-ranking official of the former KGB could make the leap and land on his feet in the GRU, much less occupy a key position of such relevance in their military establishment."

"That wouldn't have been possible in Soviet Russia," I added.

"Of course, it wouldn't! In those days the rivalry between those two Party apparatuses was fierce. More than fierce, it was brutal!" emphasized Tilson.

Andrei Kodina — now that memories from the times of the Cold War*** came rushing back — had been the chief of staff of the KGB's Atomic Fang Division, and Yuri Pavenko's immediate superior. That's why the weapon's dealer had access to state-of-the-art Russian armaments; his relationship with Kodina was the key to everything. The GRU, being the Military Intelligence Department of the Russian Army, had control over ROSOBO-RONEXPORT and now Kodina was the head.

"It's funny how the pieces are falling into place, isn't it?" grunted Tilson. "I too have been wondering all these months how Yuri managed to... Never mind, carry on, Phi."

Jessica nodded her head. She now looked radiant and very confident, and I couldn't help but reflect on my boss's natural talent for casting valuable people and putting them where they would perform best. Jessica was living proof of that. I remembered how I'd underestimated her when we first met, during Operation High Keys****, in '97, and how I'd changed my mind about her as we both faced together that diabolic alliance of Russian mobsters, Muslim terrorists and Latin American drug cartels that the Colonel had sent us out to fight later, in Colombia*****.

"Yes, sir," said my partner, "Pablo Escobar's death gave them the breakthrough they'd always sought in Colombia. They figured it would be easier for them to approach the Cali Cartel, which at first glance seemed to be made up of more civilized people with whom they could negotiate. Their strategy was evolving with the globalization of the market and all that. But the approach was unsuccessful because, although a connection was made, the first deal between the two mafias favored the Colombians more than the Russians. The Cali Cartel got a lot out of the transaction because it was able to acquire a fleet of remote-controlled midget submarines at a bargain price, imported directly from a secret arsenal in the Baltic."

"No kidding, Phi!" Tilson sneered as if he had not known any better. I suspected he hadn't.

"The lesson learned with the Colombians and with the Italians in Brighton Beach, whom they tried to scapegoat in the stolen fuel sales business, got them thinking," Jessica went on, ignoring old Al's sharp sarcasm. "Yuri Pavenko didn't like the deal the Ostrovskys intended to offer the *Cartel del Norte del Valle* in Cali. Why? Because Pavenko preferred to sell his merchandise directly to the Muslim terrorists and the drug traffickers rather than exchange it for other services or a slice of the drug market in Miami. If he sells the weapons, he gets paid, even if he is obliged to pay taxes on the earnings to the clan's higher bosses. If he exchanges them for drugs..." she paused to sketch a pout, "well, here the risk compounds, and life becomes more complicated with the increasingly difficult stage of distribution." She paused for a few seconds and turned to look at me meaningfully. "Although what you and I experienced in Colombia does not seem to support my hypothesis, Pavenko was marked to be taken out of the game by his own masters. I am *convinced* of that!"

She said it so firmly that even knowing the truth, I didn't have the strength to refute her statement; of course, I was not supposed to. Besides, describing what happened down there, the way she had, it was almost impossible to disagree. And for the second time since my boss decided to give her a position as an analyst in our outfit, I could fully appreciate how much that privileged female mind protected by an extraordinary clump of red hair —turned dirty-blond now, since she had dyed it for this operation's sake— was worth.

"What are you insinuating, Jessica? Are you telling me that Yuri Pavenko was handed over to Agent Long by his own masters?" I spat in mock bewilderment, although the image of a beaten Yuri, captured under the very noses of his own Russian bodyguards in the office of his Colombian associate by an elite OCF Moscow Bureau agent, slowly made its way into my brain******.

Tilson, who listened attentively and almost apprehensively, grumbled, and folded his arms. The situation made me more and more uneasy with every passing second. Never, in all my years as an eliminator with the Quadrille, had I ever encountered a case where a simple intelligence analyst knew more about the ongoing mission's details than the executive director in the field himself! But in this case (due to Tilson's recent transfer and promotion within the OCF, and the ambiguity with which he'd been behaving in recent times) the Colonel had denied him access to our private archives and, consequently, to the last report submitted by Phi detailing what had really transpired during Operation Scorpion Tail, as far as she knew.

"That's why The Scorpion," continued Phi grinning at me before turning to Tilson, "agreed to negotiate with the OCF; you know Arteaga represented the interests of the CIA by interceding with Pavenko for Commander Ahmed, because those two manipulated the Russian dealer to get hold of the guided missiles that the NRO man —Jack 'Bullshit' I think you called him— is after. My guess is that someone higher up in the clan's hierarchy decided that negotiating with the Islamic extremists was not in their best interest; someone with enough brains to know that once the sale of the weapons to the terrorists was discovered, both the Colombian government and the hated Uncle Sam would stick their noses into the matter. Get the picture?"

It was a great story, really, but one based only on half-truths because what Jessica did not know was that the so-called 'sale of weapons' to the Islamic terrorists was being advocated by the Colonel himself, using Pavenko, to catch them all red-handed at the time of delivery and wipe them off the map once and for all.

And that was the second time that morning I heard NRO Jack's name again, or should I say his nickname, that still unknown character who was bent on hunting down the most dangerous arm dealers on the U.S. government's blacklist. Two things happened then: first, it brought memories of another American agent with a similar mission, Mortimer Long, whom I had to put down in Colombia to —incredible as this sounds— prevent him from fulfilling it. The second thing: it made me wonder if I would have to do the same again to this Jack 'Bullshit' character....

There was a silence as thick as it was ominous. I began sweating bullets, so to speak — and so did Tilson — although for very different reasons. Jessica studied us with a blatant air of superiority, but her inflated feminist ego prevented her from grasping what that tense atmosphere and the strange attitude of my old master-instructor made me intuitively perceive. This Caribbean operation of ours was very important to *him*; it was big and ambitious, yes, because its success would be tantamount to a bite in the main artery of the Ostrovsky clan. But I could also sense that he had other motives; maybe, motives of a personal nature.

"Enough!" shouted Tilson, breaking the silence. "This is pure speculation on your part, and we are not paid to speculate. No more gossip! I have a job to do on this island and you are my tools to get it done, not my sources of information..."

"With all due respect, sir, I insist that the existence of *La sombrilla caribeña* is not gossip, but a legitimate target as it protects Russian Mafia finances from American laws," Jessica countered stiffly. "The money is laundered *outside* the U.S. Neither the Treasury Department, nor the FBI, can do anything about it! They don't have jurisdiction overseas!

That went without saying, it certainly was a black bag operation, totally illegal. That's why the Quadrille had been called in, we —as the popular saying goes— are *expendables*.

But Tilson, perhaps because he felt cornered, gave in regretfully.

"You're right, Phi, I take it back... You're right," he conceded immediately to save face, and not satisfied with his delayed reaction he turned to me and blurted out. "She is one smart operator, Delta, and *you* should follow her leads!"

In addition to surprising me by his fierce allusion to my alleged stupidity, his last remark also elicited a guffaw from Jessica.

"See, Pat?" She turned to me again and did so with delight. But then her expression changed, as if she'd picked up something that didn't add up now that we had reached the end of the sham. Nonetheless, she disguised it very well in front of Al. That made up for it. Despite reacting skillfully, our OCR had done so too late. The meeting was meant for him to be the one in charge of giving the briefing.

Tilson, get it? *Not* my partner Jessica.

*Refer to the third volume in the series, entitled *One Deadly Souk*. (*Author's Note*)
**From the Russian, it translates into English as 'mister', or 'sir'. (*Author's Note*)
***Refer to the first volume in the series, entitled *The Quadrille*. (*Author's Note*)
****Refer to the second volume in the series, entitled *Red Goliath*. (*Author's Note*)
*****Refer to the third volume in the series, entitled *One Deadly Souk*. (*Author's Note*)
******Refer to the third volume in the series, titled *One Deadly Souk*. (*Author's Note*)

*C*hapter *4*

OPERATION PARASOL

In the seventy-two hours that followed that first discouraging meeting, our routine did not deviate from the original plan. We would go out "fishing" on the high seas in the mornings, practice with the guns, and then meet with Alfred Tilson and receive new target updates; we all looked forward to the moment when we could strike. By then, the usual patterns of behavior of the sentenced mobsters were already beginning to emerge, and the team of twelve agents that old Al now had under his command, stationed on the island, was working hard to prepare an organizational chart with the comings and goings of each mark. In short, Operation Parasol was beginning to take shape before our very eyes.

By mutual agreement Phi and I selected the elimination of Goriainov as the first one. Tiger Kuzekh was second on the list, thus leaving the three bankers for last. These were labeled soft targets by Tilson's men because of the characteristics of their roles on the island. There was also a good chance that we could take them all out at once, which is known in the business as a "multiple hit."

Tilson agreed with us in general terms, but pointed out that, if we were planning to eliminate the bankers simultaneously, why not employ the same tactic with the hard targets.

"I don't see how," Phi countered, "they don't walk around holding hands, sir, they each have separate duties to perform, and they do it their own way. There's nothing in the information we have to the contrary."

"Perhaps you haven't paid close attention to my men's reports. It's clear that the two of them coincide almost daily at the fitness club, and the spa located in the penthouse. It is one of those unisex places, you know. I have already told you that Kuzekh is an inveterate womanizer who is always chasing femmes in the gym."

"Well, that's good news, isn't it?" I suddenly commented. "I just got an idea...."

"No kidding!" exclaimed Jessica, instinctively putting herself on guard. "What are you going to do, find an AIDS-infected hooker and throw her to the Tiger?"

We were amused by the way she chose to get the message across. If we were thinking of using her as a disposable concubine for that horrendous character, we might as well go screw ourselves —the both of us. But I was never serious when I mentioned my idea, it was only meant as a joke. Thus, when I caught Tilson's wily way of watching her, looking over my partner's curves with the eyes of a good taster, my blood froze in my veins.

My suspicions were confirmed when, with an indifferent shrug, old Al manifested: "I don't think it's necessary to bring in a hooker to do the job, having *you* here. I bet you can manage, Phi; you obviously have all the right attributes. I guarantee that as soon as Kuzekh bumps into you in the gym he'll go after you." He concluded with a mocking wink.

To tell the truth, at that moment I didn't know whether to laugh or shoot him.

"Motherfucker!"

Jessica burst out as soon as Alfred Tilson left. My partner was so furious that she was foaming at the mouth; just saying.

I had indeed thought of using her as bait to trap Kuzekh under those circumstances because —as our Regional Control Officer had rightly pointed out— Jessica was well-endowed for it; but never in such a risky way as he had proposed. Of course, Tilson's plan was superior to mine from a strategic point of view because it was based on dispatching the two hard targets simultaneously, an action that would decapitate the two-headed internal security apparatus of La Hacienda. But he had overlooked one very important detail: my feelings for Jessica.

"Easy, Carrots," I told her to calm her down. "The matter is not as tragic as it seems."

"God damn it, Pat, of course it is! You just say that because you are not the one he's throwing to the sharks here. Sometimes it seems I'm working with a conceited bunch of male chauvinist pigs!"

"Cut it out, Jessica! Stop acting like an amateur. Nothing's going to happen to you if I'm around to prevent it. To hell with Tilson! We'll do this our way, just you and I, that's it; but I need you willing to cooperate."

That put her in her place, though I suspect not quite, for she continued to curse Tilson's hide in an eerie low growl. I gave her time to get it off her chest. Perhaps if we played it safe, I reflected, Jessica would have no need to get in bed with Kuzekh.

"Are you carrying the pill?" I asked her suddenly.

She looked at me blankly before nodding her head. "I always do it when on a dangerous mission, why? Are you going to ask me for suicide too?"

"Oh, Jesus, don't be ridiculous, Carrots! Just got an

idea. If you manage to seduce Kuzekh and lead him to a secluded place where you can pretend to kiss him...."

There was no need to explain myself further. The idea was sketched out for her as soon as I hinted at it.

"It's still a big risk for me, don't you think? You can't pussyfoot with cyanide."

"Technically, we're paid to take risks, Phi, but if you perform the maneuver carefully it's going to be much more practical and less unpleasant than taking him to bed and killing him afterwards, when the man becomes vulnerable. I guess you know how to use that thing," I said, referring to the black pill, "you just bite down hard first and allow the cyanide to spread across your tongue before you gulp it down. You have two or three seconds for the poison to flood your mouth, before swallowing. So, you start making out with him, when he gets excited you bite down on the pill and spit it deep into his throat, if you know what I mean. Just squeeze his nostrils and grab his jaw hard, so he'll be forced to open his mouth and voilà..."

"He swallows the poison." She concluded for me.

"Exactly! Don't waste any time in distancing yourself from him as soon as he falls."

"Obviously, but I'm more concerned about being able to pull the darn thing out of its capsule behind the molar and try to shove it right down his throat than I am about what he might try do to me in his final struggles. The movement requires a certain degree of dexterity with the tongue, you know, and lots of practice."

"I know, Carrots. You could practice with me," I suggested, "but without the capsule, of course. Let's do it with a chewing gum tab."

At first, she eyed me seriously, but then a hint of jovial mischief enlivened that lovely pair of aquamarine eyes that melted my soul like ice cream under the sun.

"Yeah…" she mumbled. "Why not."

We didn't see old Al again until the day of the hit was scheduled to happen. By then I was well acquainted with the Springfield rifle and had it tuned to perfection. Phi had also spent time practicing with her new .22LR Victory SW22. It was not as compact a pistol as the pint-sized Taurus she favored, because it had the capacity to hold a much larger load. It was becoming obvious that Bill the Armorer and Col. Berkowitz anticipated so much activity in Aruba that higher shooting performance was going to be necessary on this operation.

The day chosen by Tilson was a Wednesday and already much of that week's tourist flock had left the island the day before. The incoming herd was not expected until Friday afternoon, and Tilson had made the arrangements with the FBI to have Sam Norwood — the same albino pilot who'd flown us in from Miami — on stand-by and ready to take off with us at a moment's notice if things went south. As a contingency measure, there would be a second team waiting in case Jessica and I were neutralized by the opposition. I figured the back-up crew would be made of Tilson's men. OCF people. And again, as I pondered the matter, it all came rushing back into my head. Wasn't the OCF dedicated only to the arrest and imprisonment of the criminals? Wasn't Arnold Feldman's Organized Crime Force a *law enforcement* agency — not a clandestine outfit of professional assassins, such as the Quadrille?

Hell, things still didn't add up.

Mikhail Goriainov was a man of medium height, but with the stocky build of a professional wrestler. His body had some excess fat, and that made him sweat profusely while working out on one of those weight-lifting machines. His skull was shaved military style, and a thin moustache shaped like a bicycle handlebar went down the corners of his lips, until it transformed into a goatee. He had a double chin, and his nose was short and hooked. His lively black eyes small but malevolent. In a way, the man's physical appearance reminded me of the Yuri Pavenko of yesteryear, the younger version of the man I'd met a little less than twenty years ago in New York. *

This Russian brute was dressed in sleeveless sweater and stretch pants. I watched him carefully for a while, studying the rhythm of his massive body. I needed to know how fast his reactions could be, which arm was the strongest, which leg the more powerful... and so on and so forth. Moving around the room while occasionally using the weight machines to justify my presence in the gym, I deliberately avoided looking directly into the surveillance cameras so as not to give a good shot of my face to the watchmen on duty.

As my target progressed through his work-out, I realized that this man was much stronger than I would ever be in my entire life, and the urge to own a firearm at such times of dread suddenly assailed me.

Piotr Kuzekh worked out in the adjoining room, where men and women mingled in groups participating in aerobic workouts. Kuzekh was the opposite of his colleague. Tall and lanky, his height was 6'2 and he weighed about 180 pounds. He was platinum blond, blue-eyed and had a bulbous nose, reminiscent of a clown's scarlet appendage. He was missing two front teeth, which had been replaced by gold shims.

Jessica was already in position, jumping to the music and squeals of the instructor, an effeminate mulatto, not far from her mark. Time passed. My target finished exercising his pecs and when he left the weight machines, I followed him discreetly to the showers. He stepped into the locker room and walked over to a wooden bench. With his back to me, Goriainov plopped down onto the seat; he was carrying a folded towel in his hands. It was then that I took the folding knife out of my pocket and began to approach him slyly, trying to avoid sudden movements. The Russian allowed me to get to within a few feet of him, then he turned in my direction and pulled out a compact automatic from inside the folded towel.

The barrel of the gun with which he aimed at me showed the same firmness of an accusing finger belonging to a scowling prosecutor.

"Relax, comrade. I beg you to put down that ridiculous pocketknife," he said with the same calm voice of the psychologist who tries to soothe the patient's nerves, "you won't be needing it with me."

I obeyed, of course, there was nothing to be gained by resisting at that moment and forcing the man to shoot me. To tell the truth, he'd already had plenty of time to finish me off and had not done so. It was ostensible that he wished to chat. Most of them do, anyway —at least when they think they've got you covered.

"I should have guessed it," I said, managing to put a faint smile on his lips. "I was warned that you are very competent."

"I've heard the same about you. Wasn't it you who liquidated the great Goliath?"

I looked at him without saying a word.

"You mustn't boast about it, Coonan; the Goliath you caught, assuming it was you, was not the same man as before."

"I don't know what you are talking about, of course,"

I said and returned the knife to my pocket after folding it. "I don't know of any Goliaths either."

Goriainov pointed his automatic at the wooden bench and said: "Sure. Sit down."

"Thank you".

The bench was long and narrow and the space the Russian pointed at for me to park my butt was far enough away from him to discourage any attempt to disarm him. The weapon clutched in his fist was a Spanish-made 7.65mm Llama pistol; a compact piece, which he had fitted with a silencer. It was introduced to the market in 1932, but production had not begun until the following year, manufactured by one Gabilondo & Cia. of Elgoibar, Spain. The 7.65 round —that is .32 ACP to you if you are a gringo shooter— does not have the stopping power of, let's say, a .45 ACP round, or even a .38 Special for that matter. But at this distance, I calculated, he could pierce my hide three times before I even managed to lay a hand on him.

And suddenly I realized how strange the situation had become. The gym was packed with people, yet no one else was sharing the changing room with us.

"I know why you came here, *tovarisch***," he said with a sigh of resignation. "You were sent to kill me, weren't you?"

---

*Refer to the first volume in the series, entitled *The Quadrille*. (*Author's Note*)
**From the Russian, translated into English as: 'comrade' or 'mate'. (*Author's Note*)

TARGETS WHO FIGHT BACK

Part Two

Chapter 5

ONE FRIENDLY FOE

I studied him silently, what was he driving at? A bitter smile tugged at his lips before he stated: "That's the irony of working for the big American agencies, comrade," he spat, "they never brief you properly! Not that their Russian counterparts differ from them in that respect, but you expect to at least know what's going on, so you know where you stand, don't you?" This he said, raising an eyebrow in a vague gesture that I interpreted as an act of solidarity.

Staring at him, I reflected that there must be some sort of hidden pocket in the towel he now kept folded around his neck.

"Speak plainly to me, comrade," I scowled. "*Ya nye panimayu*.*"

"There is an inordinate obsession with secrecy and security that keeps low-ranking field agents, such as yourself, always in the dark. I know you have been sent to kill me, and yet you have no idea that we are both working for the same side."

He was right about that; it never crossed my mind. Goriainov didn't belong to the Quadrille, of that I was pretty sure, but perhaps the man was one of those NOCs (no official cover) the CIA, or even the OCF itself, deploys in the field from time to time. I had run into a few of them in the recent past. On the other hand, this was not the first time in my career that someone had tried to confuse me in such a way. During the Cold War, I faced opponents who made good use of disinformation. It's a tactic that works, of course, and the Russians were always wizards at it, but there was one detail that didn't fit in this circumstance. The maneuver is always implemented by the individual whose life is in danger — in this case me — Goriainov had the frying pan by the handle. That did confuse me and prompted me to poke around for an ulterior motive behind the act, because there is always one, mind you, though I had already begun to worry more about Jessica's fate with her Russian tiger. Had things gone south for her too?

"Don't you worry about the girl, *tovarisch*," spoke Goriainov joyfully, as if he could read my thoughts. "She's in good hands. I reckon Kuzekh will be balling her while we chat. He knows your partner has orders to kill him, but that son of a bitch is madder than a goat and he's not going to take her seriously until he fucks her first... I hope she kills him!"

And that was the second sign that something didn't add up. But I kept a neutral expression on my poised face that perhaps Goriainov perceived as disbelief.

"I see that you still don't understand, or just don't believe me, which is worse. It's simple, Delta, really. Operation Parasol is not what you think. On the face of it, I am the biggest enforcer of the Ostrovsky clan on this island, but that's not the truth. I'm just a poser, comrade, a double agent if you prefer. And I don't work for the two brothers who rule this clan, my real boss is Arnold Feldman."

And if you're working for Feldman, you Russian scum, what the heck is Alfred Tilson doing here?! And consequently. *Why then are we striving to get you out of the way?* I couldn't help but think.

But since he had confessed in a tone as firm as it was chaste, it shook me to the core. The man seemed to believe what he was claiming.

"Listen, man, better make up your cotton- picking mind fast! I don't have much time to convince you," he hissed through clenched teeth and checked his wrist-watch.

"Can you prove it?" I inquired, knowing that there was no way.

"Of course not. You'll have to take my word for it. If it's any consolation, just think, you'd be dead by now if things weren't what they are. You listen well, *gospodin* Delta, Kuzekh was supposed to take your colleague to my office and screw her there. But what I have done is order him to immobilize her and keep her captive, until you and I arrive. The plan is to try to force information out of you both before we take you out, so we can determine how much you guys really know about our set-up; at least, that's what Tiger thinks. But you're going to arrive at my office alone, and with this gun," he said, surprising me by taking the Spanish semi auto by the barrel and offering me the butt. "Take this, man, take it!"

I hastened to obey him after hesitating for a moment.

"That fool doesn't suspect that I won't come to meet him. You'll be the one who does, *tovarisch*. Want my advice? If your pretty friend hasn't killed him yet, you do it."

"*Ya da panimayu,***" I sighed scratching my head. "I gather Kuzekh is in your way to some extent, isn't he?

"Yes! I've been infiltrated to undermine The Caribbean Umbrella. But I must do it the way termites work, from the inside and with a lot of patience, understand? Don't tell me now that I also must explain to you what The Caribbean Umbrella is, for God's sake!"

"Not necessary, pal," I assured him.

"Thank goodness! It's a slow process to do it this way, but it will be permanent and I'm all set for that. When I'm done here, the whole laundering operation will have been diluted and everything will go back to the way it used to be at Eagle Beach. I will not leave any of the bankers standing and I'll make sure that they will not send anyone else to take their place. Which is what will happen if you people insist on doing things the hard way. Explain that to your hard-headed chief, Coonan, you guys will just be cutting two or three tentacles off a giant octopus, while I can behead the monster."

I didn't feel like arguing anymore; he had his mission, I had mine. It mattered little to me if he truly was a double agent of the all-mighty Arnold Feldman, General Director of the OCF —the man had no business sticking his nose in our running clean-up operation. In that deadly game we were playing against the Russian Mob on a global chessboard, I'd already taken out one of Mr. Feldman's charging knights in Colombia***; why would I hesitate to take a bishop down now, here, in Aruba?

---

*From the Russian, translated into English as 'I don't understand it'. (*Author's Note*)
**From the Russian, translated into English as: 'now I understand'. (*Author's Note*)
***Refer to the third volume in the series, titled *One Deadly Souk*. (*Author's Note*)

Chapter 6

THE KILLER WITH GOLDEN TEETH

I rapped my knuckles on the door marked PRIVATE. Four quick taps and two spaced, followed by two quick ones. I didn't know for sure what awaited me inside, so I prepared for the worst.

I admit experiencing some satisfaction when the muffled shots splintered the wood. Kuzekh was not playing around, and this aroused in me a fury as deep as it was implacable. I threw a vicious kick at the door that smashed the area around the doorknob. The splintered door swung back hard, and I went in fast, crouching low and ready for anything, gun in hand. Trying to locate our Russian Tiger, the first thing I saw was Jessica's legs, slumped next to the base of a desk. The second thing I saw was Kuzhek rushing at me.

I didn't even bother to shoot him, because in the attempt to kill Goriainov I found that they had fiddled with the Llama to make it malfunction. Using it as a projectile instead, I threw it at his face as hard as I could, while simultaneously pulling my pocketknife out with one quick jerk. I think it was a matter of luck; emitting a loud thud the gun bounced off his forehead and the blood flowed. A river of ruby hue ran down his bold Slavic features, Kuzekh screamed out loud and brought both hands to his face, including the one holding a 9mm

Glock.

I rushed at him and managed to knock him down hard, but the mobster wasn't finished yet. He threw a groping elbow at my face which connected and made me bleed, too. But now he was in trouble. His problem was that exaggerated height of his. On the ground I had the advantage because his limbs were so long, he didn't have enough room to maneuver. Nevertheless, the Russian *boyevik* was strong and stubborn. He plunged a knee into my lower abdomen, which took the wind out of me. Then he tried to recoil because the blood blinded him, and he strained to wipe it off from his eyes. But I didn't let him slip away because Tiger still wielded the handgun and could shoot me at will. Grunting like a charging boar I readied the knife, by pressing the tiny button that released the blade. I embraced Kuzekh in desperation, also blinded by my own blood and rage, and groped for his torso to begin the systematic labor of plunging the honed blade again and again into his ribcage. It took five stabs. After some time, he stopped kicking and died.

Panting, I barely wiped my face and approached Jessica fearing the worst. What a relief I felt when I checked her pulse and heard her lips babble my name.

"Is that you, Pat?"

"I'm here, Carrots. The party's over," I told her, even though that wasn't quite true; we still had to escape from there.

"Did you get him? Please, tell me you got that monster…" she said in a weak, trembling voice.

"Hell, yeah; got the other bugger too. We must get out of here, c'mon!"

I helped her up and sat her down for a moment and then I noticed a laptop computer resting on the desktop, connected to a printer, and further aside a phone with a

TV screen. Suddenly I had an idea. I turned to Phi and checked that she had also picked up on the presence of the device.

"Are you thinking what I'm thinking?" she muttered.

"I think so. You feel up to it?"

She nodded her head.

"We don't have much time, Carrots," I told her, passing her Kuzekh's gun. "Here, take this just in case." She accepted the Glock and after checking to verify it was properly loaded, she put it down next to the laptop.

Jessica opened a new folder on the screen and copied as much information as possible. After that, she saved the file as Parasol, got on the Internet, and sent the document as an attachment to Mrs. Aledo's e-mail address. Then she searched through her clothes and produced a USB memory stick and inserted it into a free port on the computer.

"I just sent the data to Mrs. Aledo." She spoke. "But let me save it on my flash drive, just in case.

"How much longer, Phi?" I asked, getting a bit anxious now.

"Almost done... Look out the window, Pat. If there's water below, we can jump."

It was a relief to see that, despite the blows she had received, the girl was still lucid. As I leaned out the window my eyes met the blue waters of the kidney-shaped Olympic pool.

"You got it! We can jump." I confirmed with glee.

Chapter 7

INTERNAL CRISIS

Tilson was on the phone when we made our presence known in his office. His task force was stationed at the Seaport Village Mall on L.G. Smith Boulevard, across the bay. It was a shell company that passed for a travel and tourism agency, but the entire staff there worked for the OCF.

"What the hell happened?" He burst when Jessica and I entered his office with our clothes soaked in water mixed with chlorine and blood.

Through the office window, we could see the tower of the Crystal Casino. I looked around anxiously and found an open pack of cigarettes resting on his desk, which was kind of strange since, as far as I knew, Tilson never had any use for them.

"I thought you didn't smoke," I commented.

Tilson hung up the phone, he didn't look so happy to see us.

"They're not mine," he spat, "Sammy Norwood forgot them here. Well, are you going to tell me what the hell is going on?"

"Easy, sport; I need a stiff drink first."

"Yeah, me too!" added Jessica. "Pat, can I have a cigarette?"

I nodded my head and held one out to her.

Tilson left his desk and headed for a credenza-style cabinet, which stood behind it. He returned promptly with a half-full bottle of Scotch and three disposable cups; he also brought us a book of matches. But he looked a bit nervous, and it was ratified by the fact that he asked me to pour a drink for him as well.

"What happened?" He asked again. "Chaos has broken out at La Hacienda. We have been monitoring all phone calls and police channels and…"

"Save it for later, pal," I interrupted him sharply while still pouring whiskey into both containers. "Get the Colonel on the phone right away, dammit!

He stared at me showing a certain degree of apprehension. The man was not used to receiving this kind of treatment from subordinates.

"Wait a minute, Delta…"

"No, you bastard! You're the one who's going to wait; connect me to the Old Man *now*!

He realized it would be better for both of us to oblige and within seconds we had Col. Berkowitz on a secure line. Tilson switched him to speaker mode.

"Good evening, Delta, and Phi. I understand that you have broken protocol by overstepping the authority of the Regional Control Officer and requesting a quick conference with me. This is not a good time, I'm extremely busy… But, since we are all connected now, how can I be of service?"

"I'm truly sorry, Colonel, but something has happened that I deem to be of the utmost significance."

"Fair enough, let's hear it," he said in that casual tone he always employs on the eve of bad news.

"It just happens that this is the second time in the last few months that we've run into unforeseen interference from the other OCF divisions in the field, sir. Well, one in particular, the Moscow Bureau. I'm getting *tired* of being sent to the front lines blindfolded, you know, this must change!"

It was a well-calculated dramatic flare-up on my part, pure acting. Then I paused, to emphasize the importance of my words.

"What are you talking about, Delta?" my chief inquired.

"What am I talking about, sir...? Well, for starters, Mikhail Goriainov confessed that he was in Aruba working undercover for director Feldman and asked for my cooperation in eliminating his dangerous colleague, the second target on my list. *That's* what I'm talking about! Why am I not informed of these things, dammit! That being the case, why were we ordered to kill *him*!"

As I spoke, I refrained from looking at Tilson; that was up to Phi. In those instants we weren't sure if he was playing fair with us; or not.

"I see," we heard my boss say. "What else did Goriainov tell you, Delta, it is imperative that you be precise."

"I repeat, Colonel, he said he was an undercover agent working for Arnold Feldman; he also confessed that his mission was to go about dismantling the Caribbean umbrella from the inside. He admitted that perhaps this way it will take more time, but the effect will be permanent. Furthermore, referring to our Operation Parasol, he urged me to tell you that the way we are doing things, we would only be cutting off two or three tentacles of a gigantic octopus. Those were his verbatim words."

"Seriously?" the Colonel spoke.

"I don't buy it!" interceded Tilson. "That's the most absurd thing I've ever heard!

The Colonel paused, and a threatening silence pervaded the room; there was tension, yes, lots of tension floating in the air now. Never had Tilson dared to treat our boss as an equal. Of course, what with the new promotion and all, the Colonel no longer figured as a superior to him, not now that he was taking his orders directly from Mr. Feldman.

"By the way, how is Phi?" asked the Colonel and, although he tried, he could not entirely disguise the twitchy tone of his voice.

"She's fine, sir, and she's here listening to you; they just tossed her up a little."

"Good! Anything you want to add to that, Tilson?"

The question took old Al by surprise and made him hesitate for a moment: "No, Colonel, I'm afraid not," he answered. "I'm as surprised as the next man at what happened. We hadn't the slightest idea that they were expecting us. If so, I would have given the order to abort."

"Phi, can you hear me?"

"Yes, sir," Jessica replied instantly, "I'm here."

"Do you have anything else to add?"

"Well, we ran into luck in Goriainov's office, I accessed his database and was able to copy a bunch of files describing in detail the infrastructure of the money-laundering operation. But I have not yet had the time, nor the means, to analyze the information and evaluate it. However, we do have a flash drive with all the data in our possession. Any orders concerning the data?"

The USB stick was only a trap to deceive old Tilson. The coveted information should already be in Mrs. Aledo' e-mail. I just hoped the Colonel was aware of this. I hurried to pour another Scotch down my gullet and turned a discreet eye toward Tilson, who was swallowing dryly. I sought another cigarette from Sam Norwood's pack and lit a match to it; my brain was already working on an evasion plan, for we were to make ourselves vanish by the time Col. Berkowitz finished instructing Jessica on what to do with the information.

"Sir," I said once Phi was done with him, "I request further instructions on how to proceed."

"Why, they remain the same as before, Delta. The plan shall not be altered. Director Feldman sent you both to Aruba to conduct a clean-up mission, didn't he? Well, just wrap it up for him. That's all there is to it. He has me working on the Islamic Sword thing at the moment, and I have no news that the Moscow Bureau is conducting another covert action on the island. But I will inquire if there's something going on that I am not aware of. Carry out whatever orders are given to you by Tilson and proceed with caution. Understood?"

"Yes, sir!" I replied.

"Tilson, can you hear me?"

"Still here, Colonel."

"Clear the room, will you? I need to talk to you in private."

That was the signal I was hoping for, but when we tried to take off Alfred Tilson turned to Jessica.

"Wait a minute, Phi, you'd better leave that USB with me, I'll get some of my men to decipher the information you seized and upload it to our files, I don't want to risk losing it if anything should happen to you guys out there. Naturally," he said, raising his voice now so my boss could hear him, "I'll mail a copy of the entire contents to your inbox ASAP, Colonel."

"Yes, better do that immediately."

Jessica hesitated, looking undecided. "Are you sure you want me to hand it over, Colonel?" She raised her voice showing signs of strain. But I knew she was just pretending.

"You have *my* consent to hand over the memory stick to RCO Tilson, Phi. After all, aren't we all on the same side?" I could picture him smiling with jovial sarcasm at the other end of the line as he said this. He didn't trust Tilson any more than Phi and I did, but now was not the time to reveal our true feelings.

Tilson held out his hand as he gave us a baleful grin; he had won this little skirmish, or so he thought.

"Yes, Colonel," Jessica replied somewhat reluctantly and handed the USB to Al.

I grabbed Norwood's cigarettes and without further ado we got the hell out of there because it was becoming obvious that what my boss intended, by asking for a private audience with Tilson, was to give us a chance to vanish.

Our Caribbean assignment had entered a crisis.

*C*hapter **8**

ADRIFT

We boarded the car and the first thing we did was to look for a pharmacy. We found one called *La botica del pueblo*, where Jessica purchased a portable first-aid kit. After disinfecting the wounds and applying generous doses of an analgesic ointment for cuts and burns, we drove to the nearest AVIS branch, which turned out to be not far from Tilson's offices and exchanged our rental for a less conspicuous vehicle: a family sedan. We transferred our luggage from the red Mustang GT to our new means of transportation and merged into the night-time traffic of Oranjestad. Sometime later we left the vehicle in a dark alley behind the parking lot of the HERTZ/DE PALMA terminal and changed clothes. The used ones I cut to shreds with my pocketknife and threw them into a garbage bin.

The whole of Aruba had suddenly become a red zone for us. In theory, disengaging from Tilson's outfit accommodated us because it seemed that the man had become a part of the problem we'd come to solve, but in practice it was more difficult to close the mission without an executive director in the field to back us up with his support apparatus, of course and the Colonel was in no position to help. Well, it would be tough but not impossible.

"This is unheard of!" Breathed my partner.

"Occupational hazards, my dear," I said, raising an eyebrow as I inspected the magazines of the Victory pistols and the cylinder of the Ruger LCR .22LR double-action revolver.

"What are we going to do now?" inquired Jessica, while adjusting the strap of the armpit holster where she carried her weapon.

"I believe we should close the mission tonight; the more we wait, the better those bastards can reorganize and consolidate their defenses."

"I see your point; you expect the bankers to meet at the Florence Club. Don't you think the deaths of Kuzekh and Goriainov will disrupt their routine?"

"I doubt it; they will double their security, that's for sure, but they need to confer with each other. Those three birds have a lot to talk about, don't you think?"

"Yep, I guess you're right."

We drove our new rental through the business district, following the signs indicating how to get here and there. Fortunately, it is a municipality designed for tourism. Oranjestad is a miniature of the typical Dutch towns, with as many charms. Lots of shopping malls, all kinds of department stores and Royal palm trees artistically planted along its thoroughfares. We found a place to park near the Gaya G.F. Betico Croés Boulevard, which is the most important commercial artery on the island. We parked the car there and went shopping for more new clothes and shoes. Jessica purchased a sunhat to hide her face. We were careful to pay for everything with cash, in case Tilson had set up electronic tracking of the credit cards we carried.

At the Aruba Trading Company Jessica purchased a case of cosmetics and some hair dyes. From there we moved on to Wulfsen & Wulfsen, at No. 52 on the same street, where we purchased various clothing and other toiletries. At 9:15 p.m. we stopped for dinner at one of the local bistros. The time had come to compare notes and decide how best to end the mission.

"We should contact the Old Man before we get back to Eagle Beach," Phi pointed out, "I'm sure he has new instructions for us that he didn't want to give us in Tilson's presence."

"You bet. We can use the satellite phone we have in the car, Jessica. Hell, I almost forgot about it," I said. "I really hope the Colonel doesn't order me to go after Tilson. I've known him for many years, Carrots. Besides, the man is a tough nut to crack."

She nodded her head, while chewing a bite.

"You know," she said after swallowing, "I don't think I mentioned this until now, Pat, but thank you for saving my ass back there, at La Hacienda."

"No problem, *chiquita*. You would have done the same for me." I winked at her.

We finished dinner and, a little while later, we went about the task of renting a room in a second-rate motel.

Minutes after we had settled in, we made the phone call to Miami. As expected, it was the Colonel himself who answered.

"Delta here," I said, "is that you, sir?"

"Ah, Delta, how timely your call," he said ignoring my stupid question. "Apparently, I've uncovered a hornet's nest with my inquiries at the OCF's Washington Headquarters about a possible covert action taking place at present in Aruba by the Moscow Bureau. How about that!"

"Very interesting, sir. If only someone could explain to me why the heck is the 'Moscow Club' poking their noses in our hunting grounds? As far as I know, they haven't asked for permission to intervene, have they?"

"What's funny is that no one dares to tell me if there's something going down. In fact, the boys from the Hill reacted as if my queries were unreasonable. Of course, it's all an act, I can smell it, something big is cooking in Aruba and we've been left out. I was kind of expecting this, after your trifles in Colombia. But what really concerns me now is Tilson's odd behavior..."

He paused to prepare me before dropping the bombshell, but I was more than ready, trust me, because I saw it coming.

"The situation with Tilson has turned precarious; these things are always very unfortunate, you know. He has been with the Quadrille from the very beginning, and he was always one of my finest men."

The "*has been*" and the "*was*" made me gnash my teeth, but it didn't take me by surprise. Oh, no. Once again, it looked as if it was going to be me the one in charge of getting the dirty work done....

"Now," he went on, "I must deal with two difficult questions. One: What am I going to do with Tilson? Two: On which side, exactly, does Arnold Feldman militate?"

"Feldman? Director Feldman? Now, hold on, Colonel, I'm not getting this right... Are you insinuating that Feldman has been corrupted?"

I heard Marlon Berkowitz draw a long breath at the other end of the line. "There are certain people on Capitol Hill who think he needs to be watched. His ego is too big, as are his personal ambitions. Some even believe Feldman is capable of anything just to have his own little empire."

"His own little empire... Doesn't he already have one by sitting at the helm of the OCF? But now that you mention it, yes, I seem to have heard something from Tilson's mouth. Although he put it a bit differently."

"You heard that from Tilson?" He sounded surprised. "What *exactly* did he tell you?"

"It was sort of vague, really, something about a reform within the OCF that affected the Quadrille —well, CI5, us. I assumed you would be aware of it."

"First news! Are you saying this reform will affect us? In what way?"

I just love it when you seem to know more than they do, your superiors I mean; at least, for as long as the feeling lasts.

"Rather like we would soon stop being a pack of solitary wolves and work more closely with the Moscow Bureau... Now that I think about all this mess with Goriainov, sir, it is beginning to make more sense. Don't you think?"

"Absolutely." My boss hissed into my ear from many miles away. "So, it's true... What I was afraid of is taking place under our very own noses."

"What is that, Colonel?"

"I don't have time to explain it to you in detail now, Delta, but I promise we'll talk about this as soon as you get back. I will tell you something, though: During the first year of founding the OCF's Moscow Bureau, I was obliged to send Alfred Tilson there in an advisory capacity to the then-Director of Operations Arnold Feldman, which put him in direct contact with our man. Here's the connection between those two, but I bet Tilson didn't tell you that. At the time, the future of the Quadrille was uncertain. The DOD opted to disband us. Remember that? No one suspected that so many Soviet military and KGB agents would end up joining the ranks of the Russian Mafia."

"Sure, I remember, sir," I said. "Feldman took advantage of that bizarre request from a Deputy Minister of the Russian Federation to join forces with us and present a wider battlefront to the *Organizatsiya*."

"Fortunately for us, nine Russian Mafia clans consolidated in Helsinki, and the Quadrille was eventually revived and absorbed by the Organized Crime Force. I imagine that during those first few months that Tilson spent advising Feldman in the training of the men and women who now form his agency, a bond was established between them. I don't blame Tilson, you know; after all, who isn't afraid of unemployment?"

He paused to clear his throat loudly.

"On the other hand, I'm not in the habit of sticking my neck out for people who abandon me when the road turns thorny. If Tilson decided that siding with Feldman suited him better, that's his prerogative. We are all free to make those decisions, but there are always consequences. And for the record, there's nothing personal about this. As the Brooklyn boys say, 'you're either with us, or you're not.' As simple as that, Delta."

"The Brooklyn boys, yes, sir. I understand."

"Also," my boss went on, "I want to send a categorical message to that shmuck Arnold Feldman and all the Alfred Tilsons of this world."

"A categorical message, sir. Sure." I repeated conscientiously, knowing the sword of Damocles was about to descend.

"Let's teach him not to monkey with the axe when it's busy chopping wood. You copy, Delta? We cannot tolerate this kind of treacherous behavior in our ranks."

"Roger that, sir. I'm aware you call the shots, but this time give it to me straight, Colonel. I need to *hear* it like it is!" And I omitted that the life of a man who had served with me for many years was at stake. But he already knew that.

"Oh, don't you worry about Tilson, Delta, it may not be up to you to rub him off. I've already subcontracted another team to take care of him, but if he tries for you, or Phi, for that matter, then you both have the green light to neutralize him. Are we clear?"

"Yes, sir. Crystal clear."

"Good. Now tell me what you have arranged for tonight, do you think you can pull it off?"

"I think so, and partly with Tilson's help. It seems to me that he is going to take pains to make it easy for us now, since he needs to vindicate himself."

*C*hapter 9

TRIPPLE K

We were awakened by discreet knocking on the door. I rose grumpily and, wielding the SW22 Victory pistol, approached the door very cautiously. True, we were expecting visitors, and no truer than at the appointed time, but I hadn't made it this far alive to let my guard down now.

"*¿Quién llama?*" I whispered in my best South Florida Spanish, Cuban style. "Who's calling?" If the people outside were the same as I was expecting, they might understand me.

"*Salvoconducto,*" answered a gruff voice. It didn't sound like a young and feminine voice to me, but the password was the right one.

"*Pasaporte,*" I answered and opened the door a little, still holding the Victory semi-auto in my hand and ready to use it.

The three women scurried into the motel room, I closed the door after them and bolted it again.

"Hello, I'm Karmen, with a K," the one with the surly voice introduced herself. She was not as old as her voice suggested, but she was no spring chicken either. Karmen would have been in her forties, with a coarse face and gruff manner. "These are Kaila, with a K and Karina, with a K.

K, K, K... I thought, *like the Klu klux klan.*

"I'm Agent Delta," I introduced myself, "welcome."

At that instant Jessica emerged from the bathroom, she was wearing makeup and lipstick. She had on a red dress, very short and sexy, with one thigh exposed, and she wore a funny little bonnet on top of her fake blonde hair. The armpit holster where she carried her Victory pistol was secured around her torso. As she bumped into us, she stopped to put on a long-sleeved jacket that matched the dress and covered both the gun and the holster. It was a loose-fitting garment with padding on the shoulders, so as not to give away the presence of a concealed weapon. Her attire was completed with a pair of medium-heeled shoes in matching color. As they say in the spy films, she was dressed to kill.

I did not overlook the lascivious stare that the one called Karmen threw at her when my partner advanced towards us.

"And, this is Agent Phi," I announced. "Hey, Phi, say hello to Karmen, Kaila, and Karina. They make up the special team sent by the Colonel."

"Hi, girls," saluted Jessica and crossed her arms over her bust. It hadn't been an innocent gesture, mind you; it was meant to bring her right hand close to the butt of her pistol in case the new arrivals didn't turn out to be as friendly to us as they were supposed to be.

"I understand that you will lead us to the target," said Karina and set down the zippered duffel bag she was carrying on the floor. I noticed that the others also carried identical bags. "I'm counting on that, you know. The *pinche* albino monster who brought us here vanished without saying good-bye."

She was a funny girl, one of the naturals that make you smile —or laugh— even without meaning to. I nodded and winked at her.

"Don't you worry, mate, that's what we're here for —these your tools?" I asked, pointing to the bags.

All three nodded in unison.

"I guess they must have provided you with an image of the mark. Right?"

"They showed us some pictures; we can I.D. the mark. Do you have anything else to tell us about the target?

"Not really. Only that he's a cautious guy and has been in the trade for many years. But there is one detail you may be able to exploit."

"Such as....?" This was Karmen talking now, the one with the husky voice. Her eyes weren't looking in my direction.

"He is used to being the hunter, not the prey. He also feels protected because this is his home turf. Maybe all that makes him act a little more confident than he usually is, but don't take this for granted. I repeat this man is one tough customer."

"You think he suspects he has been marked for elimination?" asked Kaila, speaking for the first time.

"I can't be sure of that, but he probably intuits it. There's another detail, girls, he doesn't know you are here."

"That's convenient," said Karina. "Well, we are ready now."

"Okay. Just give me a few minutes to change."

In the bathroom I freshened up my face and dressed in a black sweat suit. I refastened my armpit holster strap with the Victory and tucked away the Ruger .22LR revolver in its ankle holster. Now all I was missing was my communication gear.

"Listen up," I told them, when we met again, "we are going to take you to the designated site. The mark should be barricaded in his office, not far from here. If that's not the case, you will have to sit tight and wait for his return. Did you bring comms devices with you?

"We came prepared," said Karmen, and knelt next to her duffel bag to open it and rummage inside. As she did so, I looked at the others in her company. Karina, who seemed to be the captain of the team, was a monument of a woman: jet-black hair and cinnamon skin; of medium height with a solid, curvy body. She looked in very good health. Kaila was not exactly a beauty, but she looked much nicer than her partner Karmen. At last Karmen stood up with a radio transmitter and looked Phi in the eye before she held out the device to her. None of the people in the room overlooked the symbolic gesture, but Jessica smiled mischievously when she took it, and then slowly handed it over to me.

Minutes later we were boarding our rented sedan.

We dropped them in front of the Crystal Casino, at the center of L.G. Smith Boulevard. I stopped the car in an alley that stood on one side of the busy street and showed them exactly where the Seaport Village Mall was. There were no more questions after that, and we watched them vanish into the gloom of that cool Caribbean night. Jessica and I resumed our journey to Eagle Beach. We were already half a mile away when Karina's voice came through the transmitter.

"This is K-1 calling Delta. We have located the site and are already in position. Over." She spoke.

"This is Delta. Roger that," I replied. "If all goes well, you will be hearing from us in a couple of hours. Happy hunting until then. Over and out."

After that brief exchange we headed down Time-Share Lane. Eagle Beach is located on the southwestern coast of the island, which forced us to proceed northbound, as Oranjestad lies a bit further south. On the way we had to cross Divi Beach in Druif Bay, enter through Manchebo and make a turn of almost one hundred and eighty degrees. Until very recently this place had been nothing more than a beachy wilderness with a few hikers' shacks on either side of the road. But that was before the Russian Mafia took it upon themselves to set up The Caribbean Umbrella. Today Eagle Beach has become one of the busiest tourist centers in the region.

We finally arrived in front of a neon sign announcing the Casino Royal Hacienda —sounds familiar? We pulled into the parking lot and found a vacant space to park.

"This handgun might be a marvel and all you want, but it's very uncomfortable to carry around," my partner grumbled.

"Uncomfortable?" I questioned her. "C'mon, Jessica, it may be a little bulkier than that Brazilian miniature you're used to, but it's way ahead of it in accuracy and shooting capacity, or are you going to deny it? The difference lies precisely in the length of the barrel and its longer magazine."

"It is a pain in the ass! Besides, the armpit holster ruins my figure!"

"Dammit, Carrots. You look *so* sexy in that little red dress; I'd gladly screw you right here and now."

"Be careful what you wish, big mouth..."

Ignoring the enticing tone of her voice, I tried to focus on the mission ahead. I unzipped one of the duffel bags and pulled out a couple of radio transmitters. I handed one to Jessica and tuned the one I kept for my personal use.

"What frequency are you on?" she asked, as she tried to calibrate her piece. I gave her the frequency; she tuned it in and slipped the radio transmitter into her purse.

I grabbed a bulletproof Tac-Vest and covered my plexus. I used the side pockets to store the .308 cartridges for the Springfield rifle, two extra clips for the Victory, and three drum loads of eight .22 Long Rifle cartridges for the Ruger. The knife remained in one of the pockets. I unzipped the bag and reached for the suitcase containing the rifle.

"You know," I commented, "I never thought that someone of Arnold Feldman's grade would be capable of...."

"The Colonel says he always suspected it."

"Well, he knows the man better than us, but still, this is all so illusory... We're not talking about a simple special agent here, for Christ's sake. We're talking about the *general director* of the OCF himself!"

"That's right, and now Tilson." She added.

"And now Tilson," I said, "what a run we've had! Well, the time has come for us to part, Carrots. Don't you do anything foolish, eh? Your role tonight is as a scout, the gun is just a precaution. You locate the targets, pass the information on to me, and I'll take over, you copy?"

"Roger that. But what if I run into Tilson in there?"

I let out a sigh. "That's not supposed to happen, but if it does, you take him out."

"Just like that?"

"Listen to me, *chiquita*," I hissed grabbing her by an arm. "Don't you make the mistake of dithering with him! Tilson won't give you time to make amends, you hear? Now be a good girl and get on with it. And don't forget, I'll be on the roof."

"Okay, *chiquito*." She answered mimicking my voice.

Chapter 10

DRINKS, CIGARS, AND BULLETS

Twenty minutes later I was lying face down on one end of the roof of the Casino Royal Hacienda. From the heights, with a black balaclava covering my head, I controlled everything through the telescopic sight equipped with a special lens for night vision. The images were somewhat ghostly as they were captured in greenish hues. I unlatched the rifle bolt and inserted the first .308 cartridge into the chamber. There was a handful of them next to me, ready for when the time came. *Step aside, Jackal*, I thought facetiously, evoking the famous literary creature by English novelist Frederick Forsyth, *here comes Agent Delta!*

A few minutes later, and still not hearing from Jessica, I experienced abrupt urges to smoke but restrained myself. I popped a piece of chewing gum into my mouth and did my best to ignore the calls of the vice. The breeze was blowing in from the beach. Across the street, at the other end of the kidney-shaped building, was the Florence Club. I watched the people moving back and forth through the glass windows. Some were chatting around the bar; others were holding onto their glasses and cups, leaning against the partitions; others drank at the tables.

By then I had Jessica located — she was seated near

the stage. Most of the men were dressed in tuxedos; some in all black, others in white dinner jackets and red bow ties. The look of wealthy people, accustomed to luxury, abundance and the typical glamour of the jet-set community who dwell in the high life, was prevalent. They gesticulated with grandiloquence when conversing among themselves, drinking good Scotch, and puffing on ostentatious *Cohibas* like the *nouveau riche*, very sure of themselves, of their financial achievements and the piles of gold and silver ingots they all kept in their bank's vaults.

What a pity not to show all those well-dressed whippersnappers how vulnerable they were!

When the Russian bankers made their appearance, I recognized them on the spot. All three were burly, nervous men. Krakov was the bald one with the thick glasses and flabby cheeks. Ismailova, short in stature, but excessively thick, with bushy eyebrows that harmonized with a Cossack's mustache in the shape of a bicycle handlebar. Bronsoski was the tallest of the threesome and as hairy as a grizzly bear. Through the magnifying lens of the Springfield's scope, the Russians appeared to be so close that I could almost brush them with my fingers.

My wristwatch read 01:27, when I began to wonder how Karina and her girls were doing back in Oranjestad. I checked my watch again and returned my right eye to the scope. I could see Phi well across the street now, she was struggling with her purse, and I got a feeling she was about to transmit. I wasn't wrong.

"This is Phi calling Delta. Do you copy? Over."

"This is Delta. I hear you loud and clear, Phi. Over."

"Are you in position? Over."

"Affirmative. Over."

"They're all here. Do you have a visual? Over."

"The three chickens in the pot... Any signs of the Old Rooster himself? Over."

We both knew I was referring to Tilson.

"Negative. I'm on my way out now, you've got the green light. Over and out."

"Roger that. Over and out," I repeated after her before switching off the comm. I set the transmitter next to me on the roof and focused on the scope once again.

It was then that things began to happen. I felt the short hairs on the back of my neck stand erect under the elastic fabric of the balaclava and a very unpleasant feeling ran up and down my spine. I reacted by looking up just in time to catch a metallic glint that pierced the darkness. This happened at roof level, in the building across the street, on a wing parallel to my location. The rooftop of the Florence Club! My ears picked up the faint but ominous raking of an automatic weapon. It's a very peculiar dry click, as unmistakable as a death sentence.

Across the street, merged with the shadows of the roof, an unknown shooter was getting ready to open fire on me.

There were two of them; I realized that as soon as another burst of gun fire rained down over my position. Lead whizzed around me, and the hot fragment of a ricochet embedded itself near my left hip.

I grunted and returned fire with one crummy single shot from the Springfield — that miraculously managed to hit one of the triggermen. Not having time for more, I abandoned the rifle on the roof and limped for cover behind the massive external a/c unit. My next step was to get my hands on the transmitter and update Jessica on my current situation.

"What's going on, Delta, these people are still stand-

89

ing! Over." She hissed over the set when I contacted her.

"I've been made, Phi. I repeat, I'm in no condition to do the cooking. You must do it for me, you copy? I repeat: The kitchen floor is all yours now. If I'm not waiting for you in the car when you get back, don't wait for me... Good luck. Over and out."

I hated myself for doing that to her, but what choice did I have? Without the Springfield there was no chance of completing the mission.

The surviving shooter ceased firing. It was obvious that he had access to a night vision device of some kind because his shots had passed by very close. In the dark, I probed my wound with two fingers and felt blood oozing from it that made me curse under my breath. To escape the ambush, I had to reach the fire escape ladder and leave the roof by that route. Jumping from that height was not plausible. I bit my tongue and limped some more. More muffled shots followed close on my zig-zagging trajectory. Another piece of hot lead grazed my left elbow, but by then I had already reached the metal staircase and was sliding down it.

I gasped my way to the ground and hid behind a huge metallic garbage depository. The nauseating smell of rotting food mingled with all kinds of stench. For an instant I was about to faint, my elbow wound was also bleeding and, although superficial, I was now limping around writhing in pain. I stopped for a moment to see if I could detect any sounds, but nothing was moving. Then I heard an acute shriek, and a cat jumped out of the darkness, landing right into the garbage dump, almost giving me a heart attack.

I turned with a start and raised my SW22 Victory, looking for a target. I couldn't see any pursuers, but I could imagine who they were. The goddamned *boyeviks*, the overtrained enforcers of the Russian Mafia who were part of the security corps stationed at La Hacienda. I set course for the car, hoping that I could get to it before Phi, when the world suddenly changed...

"Hold it right there, buster!" shouted a familiar male voice. "And drop your weapons!"

The threatening tone of his demand stopped me dead on my tracks as it rumbled like thunder out of the night.

"Drop the gun, Pat. You know I'll shoot you if you make me. The party's over!"

Tilson... Son of a bitch!

I must have been in bad shape to let him get the best of me so easily.

"I'm aiming a loaded shotgun at your gut, tough guy, you don't really want to push your luck, not with this cannon at this distance. Right?"

He was right, of course; a shot from such a weapon in such close quarters could not miss.

"If you behave yourself, you won't get hurt. I give you my word. Phi seems to be managing very well by herself up there. I can hear the gunshots, can't you?"

No, dammit, I couldn't hear them, and besides, his own voice seemed to be drifting farther and farther away from me, dragging my consciousness out of my body. A wave of nausea took me by storm. I stumbled and Tilson stepped aside with the grace of the big felines, probably thinking it was a ploy. The SW22 slipped from my hand, and I contracted, waiting for the gut-wrenching blow of the shotgun blast that never came.

"Easy, Pat!" Tilson hissed.

But nothing mattered to me anymore. The earth was beginning to spin frantically around me, and suddenly I felt very tired.

Fuck'em all! I thought, already about to cross that feeble border that separated me from the abyss. It seemed I was on my way to hell.

THE TURNCOAT
Part Three

*C*hapter *11*

TAKE THE MASK OFF

I woke up in the office of our Regional Control Officer for the Caribbean, feeling both fragile and depressed. It was a strange feeling, one of total abandonment, which I never recall having experienced during an operation. Tilson was kneeling beside me, busy stopping the flow of blood from my injured elbow. I noticed that he had already applied a tourniquet to my hip —a primitive first-aid job— that had successfully stemmed the bleeding.

"There," he said as he applied the final touches to the bandage on my elbow. "How are you feeling?"

"Bad," I replied. "What time do you have?"

He glanced at his watch; I didn't have the strength to check mine.

"It's 02:13, Pat," he said nonchalantly.

"Where is Phi?" I asked. "Did she make it? I must know!"

"Easy, lad, don't torment yourself. Looks like she made it," he said and went to his chair behind the desk. "She's been trying to reach you through that piece of junk."

Thank God! I thought but struggled not to show my relief.

Believe it or not, I was still not sure how to deal with

Tilson. His performance was certainly ambiguous; first he betrayed us with Goriainov and Tiger Kuzekh, then the bastard ambushed me at the whereabouts of the Florence Club and threatened me with a shotgun, but now he was bandaging my wounds... A puzzle.

"Make up your mind, Al," I said, playing hard to get now. I was trying to provoke a reaction that would give me a clue, "you're either with us, or you're not."

I watched him sneer and turn to open the doors of the credenza-style cabinet and pull out a bottle of whiskey. He also produced a couple of disposable cups and filled them. Tilson held one out to me and sat back down behind the desk.

"So now you're quoting the Brooklyn boys too, huh? Ha! It feels like I'm listening to the old devil himself!" And then he grinned, raising his cup. "Cheers."

I watched him deliberately in silence and took a sip. The whiskey burned my esophagus, but it also gave me courage. It must have been that bad Irish blood we had in common. His grin widened as he noticed the revitalizing effect the good Scotch had on me. Then he refilled my cup.

"The Colonel is just a stubborn, narrow-minded Polack who tends to see everything in black and white, a 'shitty little Pole,' as old Landon used to call him, but the truth is not so hunky-dory, Pat," he added. "Do you have time for a little chat?"

"Do I? You're the one pointing the barrel of the gun at me, remember?" I commented in response to his friendly sarcasm.

"You know, don't think it's easy for me to get started. After all, I've been with the Quadrille for much longer than I care to remember," he paused to take another sip.

"May I light a cigarette?" I asked and he nodded in that condescending way professional executioners tend to grant the last wish of a death row inmate.

Very carefully, I removed the "forgotten" by Norwood pack from one of my Tac-Vest pockets and showed it to him. Tilson gave me the thumbs up by slowly nodding his head again. I looked for my lighter to light a cig and couldn't find one, it was then that I realized he had stripped me of all the metal objects I'd been carrying. A feeling of helplessness came over me as I realized that, if Karina and her girls tried to communicate with me through the transmitter, the man before me would hear it.

"My lighter?" I asked.

He reached for it and, after studying it well enough to convince himself that it did not conceal a flamethrower, handed it over to me.

"Twenty-two years, geez!" he exclaimed. "It's said fast, but it's a lifetime. I've given my best years to Col. Berkowitz and his damn Quadrille. I could dare say the same about our government and our country, because I put in ten with the CIA, but that doesn't seem to count. We're a bunch of outlaws, aren't we? There aren't many politicians who approve of our existence; you know that. In fact, they don't even have the guts to admit in public that we exist... *We* are the garbage collectors of this great nation of ball-less hypocrites who only preach 'political correctness' but *hide* everything else!!"

A brief pause to catch his breath before he continued in a harsh tone:

"We are the rug sweepers of America, Pat. Very necessary, mind you, to keep our cities clean and safe for the taxpayers, but deep down we suck up all the muck we have to deal with and, most importantly, we have blood on our hands, so no one in their right fuckin' mind would ever think of inviting us over to a home dinner. But things have changed in recent times with the rising

97

of the Russian Mafia as a global crime syndicate, and, of course, the emergence of Islamic Sword, which has led to the reorganization of the OCF. Long live the anonymous heroes! Damned whippersnappers."

The bitterness accumulated over the years was beginning to well up in the depths of his chest. A fissure that seemed to widen more and more had begun to crack the dam that contained turbulent waters about to burst. The one who thus spoke now was not the old Alfred Tilson I had known and respected in my youth, my Quadrille instructor, this was a man gnawed by the cancer of resentment and soured by the blows dealt to him by life. And I never realized how affected I was by those very same blows, until I started listening to him rant like this.

"Where is all this leading us, Al?"

"Where does it lead? Shut up and listen, you bloody idiot!! If you're sitting comfortably in that chair, smoking, drinking and still breathing it's because of the good will of a man named... well, let's call him Mr. F for now, shall we?"

"Feldman?" I grinned. "Or Fu Manchu?

"I said Mr. F. It's he who has a message for you," how ironic can life gets, I thought, because I had one for him as well, "and I'm supposed to be the one to deliver it. Mr. F has noticed you, my dear Patrick, because in all the joint operations you have participated in, you always end up depriving him of his valuable human resources. You've caused more problems for him than the ones you've solved."

"And you, Al, are you also one of Mr. F's valuable human resources?

"From now on yes," he admitted, "and listen to me well. I have been authorized to tell you that Mr. F is aware that you've been in the business of screwing him from the very beginning. Your first victim was Marvin Rose* in Key West, during Operation High Keys; then you screwed Mortimer Long** in Colombia, Operation Scorpion Tail, remember?" he paused to give me a deadly glare, "and *now* you just did it once more, here, in Aruba. Mikey Goriainov. That's three out of three, my dear Patrick, *three*."

"And the third time is the charm, right?"

"That's how it goes, yes," he said with a hard grin.

"Well, you can assure your Mr. F that there's nothing personal about it, my *dear* Al," I recited, mimicking his New England accent, "or you forgot I just follow orders?"

He sighed with resignation before countering.

"That's precisely the problem, Pat: your bloody orders. Mr. F suspects that it was you, following orders *not given* by him, who took out Mortimer Long. Forgive me if I get the names mixed up, I didn't know the guy. Like I said, I'm just passing on the message."

"You got the name right. But Mr. F is wrong, Al, I had nothing to do with Morty's death!" I lied. "The kid was too smart for his own good, he went after Pavenko and his Colombian partner solo, he didn't want to share the glory of success with the rest of us, and it got him killed. Long died at the hands of one of Yuri's thugs."

"Save your breath, man, the details don't concern me. You'll have to explain it to Mr. F, not to me. He thinks you've got something against him, and you've been knifing him in the back with full intent. That may be so, but we're all aware that you're nothing but a well-trained mastiff of your Machiavellian boss."

"And are you not?" I fired back at him.

"Oh, yes," he smiled, "I was once, too. But that's already in the past. Anyway, here goes Mr. F's message to you: you can die right here, right now, or..."

"Or what?" I cut him.

"Or you agree to become part of the mechanism. You must fill the vacancies you've caused."

"Well, I should have guessed it. An eye for an eye. In other words," I said, "it's *plomo o plata*, lead or silver, isn't it?"

"In other words, I'm afraid it is. See? You learn fast."

I stared at him sharply, while mulling over my thoughts; in the end, still unable to believe what I'd just heard, I shook my head back and forth before saying:

"I don't get it. What's wrong with you, Al, have you lost your mind? Are you really leaving us?"

Tilson smiled bitterly.

"You are a fool," he said, "if you don't accept our offer. Marlon Berkowitz and his Quadrille are done," he paused to shrug his shoulders. "Times are changing, Delta. There is a unification movement set in motion; we can no longer operate as lone wolves, outside of a central directive. The Cold War, as we knew it, ended more than ten years ago, wake up, lad, the times of 'dinosaurs in trench coats' are over. Only you and your boss don't seem to accept it."

I was blinded by rage when I heard him speak that way. "What exactly are you talking about?"

"Saving your ass, you sucker! Join us, for Christ's sake; you can't keep doing your little Colonel's dirty work forever! Look, Pat, the offer we're making to you is for you alone; Jessica stays out of this. As a matter of fact, she will serve as the sacrifice goat. We'll let her die during the mission to atone for your sins."

"My sins?"

"Yep. Those three good OCF agents you knocked off. And that's that. So, you tell me now, old boy: Are you with us?"

Many things I didn't understand before began to

make sense at that moment. My instinct made me see that Tilson's betrayal, if we could call it that, was a well-planned move that had been underway for quite some time now. Probably since the very day I disposed of Agent Marvin Rose, back in the Florida Keys. Or since that episode in Colombia with Mortimer Long, Yuri Pavenko and his partner The Scorpion, who knows.

I tilted my head to look him in the eye while simultaneously measuring the distance and the angle that separated him from the only window in the room, but the odds were not good.

Where the hell were the Triple K operatives? All I could think about was them!

But Tilson kept pointing my own gun at my torso and judging by the firm grip he had on the SW22 Victory, I could tell he was ready to use it. Understanding this did me good, it relieved me of the burden of conscience I felt from having to kill him or assist others to do it for me.

"Ok, champ, what is it going to be?" he urged me.

"I don't know, dammit! I'm overwhelmed!" I spat to buy more time. "I don't know Feldman enough to trust him. Besides, you haven't talked to me about compensation, yet."

He grimaced and gulped down the rest of the whiskey.

"You *don't* need to know him well. You'll be working with me; I'll be the one to direct you. As for your slice of the pie, well, I'll tell you there's a lot of dough involved. This is a thriving business and the best thing about it is that the big bucks you will receive in return for your loyalty and services are not American taxpayers' money and will come to you tax free. We are going to open a little savings account for you right here, in a bank in Aruba, I can even arrange a transfer for you to come officially under my command, now that you have caused me a vacancy with your silly sniper rifle; as I told you at the beginning, the Quadrille's days are numbered."

There was a brief pause to fill in his lungs, and then: "You're not a spring chicken anymore, Pat, how old are you; forty, forty-five? You may have saved a few thousands, but at the rate you're going you won't live to enjoy it; think about it... Shit, no more whiskey!"

He left the chair mumbling and took a few steps in the direction of the credenza, where he kept his liquor. At no time did he turn his back on me, not even once, as he reached for another bottle of Scotch. The SW22 semi auto was still clutched firmly in his right hand.

Where the hell were Karina and her team!!!

*Refer to the second volume in the series, entitled *Red Goliath*. (*Author's Note*)
**Refer to the third volume in the series, entitled *One Deadly Souk*. (*Author's Note*)

Chapter 12

THE AXE THAT CHOPS WOOD

My self-preservation instinct forced me to jump on the desk and try to seize the Ruger he had taken away from me, or the pocketknife, which now rested on the surface of his bureau. But an inner voice warned me that I would never make it, not with Tilson as an adversary, who was a veteran in the killing arts. The shotgun was out of my reach, he had left it leaning against the far wall.

Then I saw the beam coming out of nowhere like an unexpected miracle. A thin halo of red light landed like a silent wasp on old Al's broad back, sliding down it until it stopped right at the center of his shoulder blades.

"What you have revealed to me," I said to keep him distracted, "is quite shocking. Wow... you certainly have blown me away. Peculiar, isn't it?

"Jesus, I could have sworn I had *another* bottle!" He snapped. "Did you say 'peculiar'? *What* is peculiar?"

"The message you just passed on to me: *That* is peculiar. The reason I find this odd is because someone else also gave me a message for you."

This made him pause in his search for alcohol and tune up his ears, like a stalking Doberman. I prayed to God that he would not turn to face the window now. I had to keep all his attention focused on me.

"You are a funny guy," he said with a twisted grin. "What message are you talking about, Patrick?"

"The one sent to you by a gentleman named... Well, let's just call him Mr. B."

"Mr. B? Oh, I get it, you mean your boss, the Colonel?" He said and the grin evolved into a grimace. "Well, he can go rot in hell!"

"Do you want to hear what he has to say, or not?" I persisted in keeping him busy.

"Sure, why not, spit it out, lad... Now, where the *fuck* is that bottle, dammit!"

The red dot oscillated slightly, and I realized I'd better hurry, or pretty soon he wouldn't be in shape to hear me out. Whoever was behind the scope out there was calculating the distance of the shot against the wind speed, the angle of the gun's position and the force of the rifle's recoil. I had no idea what gun they were using, and I really didn't care if they could hit the mark.

"Come on, sport, spit out your little message. What did the old fox order you to tell me, huh?"

"Here you go, *sport*," I said, mimicking his odious New England accent to perfection, "you must learn not to monkey with the axe..."

My timing was perfect.

The window cracked at first but then it exploded into a myriad shard. Next came the noise of the glass shattering, and it made me jump.

One shot was all it took, just one. It really was a spectacular performance. One moment Tilson was standing in front of the cabinet, and the next instant he was lying sprawled on the floor. I'm sure the man never knew what hit him. The sniper's bullet pierced his spine, ripping his soul away from his body in a flash.

For a few moments I felt sorry for the man who, although he'd become a traitor, was one of the most solid pillars on which my formation in the Quadrille was based. I recalled him standing tall, his back erect and a self-assured grin brightening his features next to Col. Berkowitz in front of the entire class, that night when he addressed all recruits for the first time to tell us about his unconventional specialty.

"My assignment" he began "is to teach you all how to kill in cold blood and up close," he told us matter-of-factly, "in the trade it's called *wet work*. I am familiar with all your curriculums, and I know your backgrounds very well; I also know that some have already killed from afar using a long-range weapon, but it is not the same... Others have killed in self-defense, but that is an animal act of preservation and, I repeat, not the same either... Death on demand is a science, ladies, and gentlemen. First it must be envisioned, then well-planned, and finally executed. It can, and often does, become a botched job in the hands of neophytes, but I have known many experts in the field who have transformed contract killing into a sublime act, to be executed with mastery and pride. Like a matador's cape pass without the crowd shouting *Olé*."

Like a matador's cape pass... without the crowd... shouting Olé... I mumbled slowly to myself.

"This is K-1 calling Delta, do you copy? Over."

Those words, mixed with radio static, brought me down from the cloud. I drew a long breath and shook my head to dispel the last memories that had made me evoke the life of that formidable warhorse that had been Alfred Tislon, and I finally reached for the transmitter.

"This is Delta, K-1, come in. Over."

I released the transmit button to activate the receiver and anxiously awaited a response.

"I need your report on the situation, is the target down? Over."

I filled my lungs with air and exhaling another long sigh I approached Tilson's corpse. It was a sight as morbid as it was grotesque, even for someone like yours truly, here, someone used to look at death in the face."

"Affirmative. Your mission has been accomplished. I repeat: the target is down. Do you copy? Over."

"Roger that. K-1 signing off. Over and out."

Her voice trailed off and for a few moments I remained standing motionless over the corpse of the man who had betrayed us. I contemplated his broken shape for a few seconds more. My throat felt dry, as weariness sank in. Then I swallowed hard to find my voice again and concluded reciting my boss's message intended for Alfred Tilson.

"You should have learned not to monkey with the axe, sport, when it's busy chopping wood."

Chapter 13

READY FOR EVAC

Everything went smoother after that. I contacted Sam Norwood through my transmitter and asked him to rush to Tilson's office. He seemed to be expecting my call and assured me he would be here shortly. I told him to bring along a cleaning crew.

"Will do, Pat, and congratulations," he said before signing off, "you're on your way to becoming CI5's new OCR for the Caribbean. Over and out."

"Yeah, right," I mumbled and then cut off.

To know that Sam was on his way was a warranty of success. He was the kind of guy who always did what he said he would. Rain or shine, you could always count on his word. Even in the middle of a revolution or an earthquake, through the dust of the settling debris Sam would show up.

But then I remembered Jessica....

My nerves kicked in and, again, I grabbed the transmitter. I kept trying to contact her in vain until someone knocking on the door made me desist. Not being one to leave weapons strewn about, I picked up the SW22 Victory automatic from where it had fallen and reached for my pocketknife and the Ruger. I secured the revolver in one of the many Tac-Vest compartments and tucked the pocketknife in one of my pants' lateral pockets. Then, with the Victory ready, I set out to open the door very cautiously.

"*Salvoconducto...*" a woman's voice hissed from the other side.

"*Pasaporte.*" Was my dry reply, and I stepped aside to let them in.

The three girls slid by me carrying their gear without noise, like panthers moving through the night.

"Your evacuation is already in motion," I told them. "I'm waiting for reinforcements; you will be going home soon. By the way, congratulations on a job well done... Which one of you took the shot?"

"Me," Karina said, "today was my turn. We rotate."

"I see," I said and looked her in the eye. Unable to help myself, I held out a hand to her. She stared at it in amazement, hesitated for a second, but then held out hers to me and we shook them with professional camaraderie. I think she liked the gesture, but I could be wrong. Some pros just take you for a sentimental fool.

Norwood and his clean-up crew arrived faster than I expected. I called him aside for a brief private conference and, among other things, asked him if he knew anything about Phi. Jessica was aware that in case of an emergency she should contact Sam. Norwood admitted to having spoken to her while *en route* to meet me, just a few minutes earlier. My partner had informed him of the success of her mission, which meant that the Russian bankers were all dead and that she had managed to escape the slaughterhouse alive.

Screw you, Tilson!

Well, that was the good news. The bad news was that Jessica had been wounded in the process and she was unable to reach our escape vehicle. The bulk of the Russian Mafia hardmen in Aruba had now taken to the streets in hot pursuit and were combing the area searching for her.

A real manhunt.

Sam promised to do everything possible to extract her from the red zone, before the authorities blocked the island's main roads with barricades. Luckily for us, the police in Aruba don't move as quickly as they do in the States, but we did expect them to react in some measure within a reasonable amount of time. Now, the most serious threat came from the Russian *boyeviks*.

I didn't hesitate to join my partner's rescue effort, even though I was not in the best shape to do so; the loss of blood had drained most of my energies, but nerves and adrenaline are very powerful agents that compensate in situations like this. Don't forget that it was *my* woman who was in danger out there, and to hell with the Colonel if he didn't approve of my actions, since they totally disobeyed his arbitrary rules of professional conduct.

I remember reaching for the dead Tilson's shotgun. Sam stopped me on my way out, but it was only for a moment to hand me the keys to his SUV and to emphasize that if I didn't feel up to it, he already had his people working on getting Phi off the hook. But he understood my motives without further explaining on my part and gave me an encouraging pat on the back.

"*Vaya con Dios*, Delta," he said at last, before reassuring me that he would follow me in another vehicle with agents Greenwald and Benson, and that no effort would be spared to rescue Jessica.

Rolling down Time-Share Lane, I struggled with my heightened emotions and controlled the urge to floor the gas pedal. Every second that passed without me reaching her side brought Jessica closer to a final meeting with the Grim Reaper. The vehicle Norwood lent me was one of those massive SUVs manufactured by Dodge, the Durango model. A true monstrosity with four-wheel drive, an engine designed to fly low and a chrome-plated solid body suitable for tearing down brick walls.

I lit a cigarette to calm my nerves as I drove down the highway towards Eagle Beach. After a few minutes I tried to contact Jessica via transmitter and got lucky.

"Delta!" she breathed, "you have no idea how glad I am to hear your voice! Where are you now? Over."

"I'm coming for you, Phi! Hang on a few more minutes, I'm almost there. Confirm your location. Over."

She did and I verified that it was still the same one Sam had passed on to me. Jessica started guiding me toward her position through the radio, as I got closer her voice became clearer. She'd hidden on the seashore. Eagle Beach is lined with rock formations that allowed her to stay out of sight of her pursuers, the problem was the dogs.

The entrance to the beach was guarded. A pair of BMWs, occupied by sour-faced, heavily armed men in plain clothes, waited on either side of the road. None of them looked like OCF agents to me; quite the contrary. But I didn't intend to come in shooting like a crazy cowboy and blow it all to hell. They would make mincemeat out of me because they were packing enough firepower to fight a small war. Maybe I should have let Norwood, and his Bureau titans handle Jessica's extraction, but it was too damn late for second thoughts now....

They were all over me.

"*Piristavat!*"* These guys were so absorbed in their search that they shouted at me in Russian. A burly young man dressed in a sweat suit and tennis shoes jumped out of one of the BMWs and approached me, he was wielding an UZI submachine gun.

"Halt!" He shouted again and got in my way, forcing me to hit the brakes. I stopped the big SUV and made a visual scan of my surroundings, just in case Jessica was nearby. It was at that instant that my damsel in distress appeared, I had given her the vehicle's description over the radio, anticipating exactly what had happened.

The Russian barked another order in his native language, but since I was not supposed to understand it, I pretended not to.

Hoping to confuse the mobster, I riposted in what I consider my best Spanish: *"¡Qué bicho lo ha picado, hombre!**"*

The young *boyevik* came to stop a few feet away from the Durango's windshield and raised the barrel of his UZI submachine gun in an ominous way. I feigned panic at the sight of the SMG and raised both arms in one swoop, just as any innocent tourist would have done. Then I sensed some bustle to my right and my blood chilled in my veins —it was Jessica, and she was running towards me.

Someone inside the BMW started shooting with a high caliber pistol by the sounds of it.

I immediately understood that it was time to act, because the bugger with the UZI had also caught the movement and was now turning his body in the direction of my partner with his submachine gun at the ready. I switched on the high beams, blinding all of them momentarily. The maneuver worked and Jessica gained more ground without being mowed down by the mobsters' bullets, it was when she almost reached the SUV that the closest Russian thug rushed forward to stand between her and the Durango's passenger door. I couldn't help what happened next, it was pure reflex action.

I reversed the car a bit, turned the wheel around and ran him down.

Chapter 14

ALL HELL BREAKS LOOSE

Unable to get in the cabin, Jessica climbed as best she could into the cargo bay of the SUV. Turning the steering wheel to the left, I accelerated, and the rear wheels of the vehicle ran over the unfortunate mobster who had gotten in our way. A barrage of lead poured down on us, shattering the rear window of the vehicle. And, suddenly, the BMWs were on the move.

"Are you all right, Phi?" I asked my partner.

"I think so!" She shouted back, but I could see she was bleeding from a thigh wound.

"Here, grab this and do what you can to keep them at bay!"

I passed her the shotgun and turning the wheel left and right I managed to get back on Time-Share Lane. Out of the corner of my eye I could see Jessica working the lever of the Browning before moving to the rear end of the vehicle. She took cover as best she could and began firing. The loud reports issued by the Browning were hellish music to everyone's ears. In the rearview mirror I watched as the hood of the nearest car popped, leaving the vehicle smoking and zigzagging in a drift. I floored the accelerator making the tires screech.

We began to put some distance between ourselves and our pursuers. The Browning roared again as I reached for the transmitter. My first attempt to communicate with Sam Norwood failed, perhaps because the equipment was faulty or out of range. Then I reached for the car phone and turned to my partner.

"Quickly, Phi!" I yelled. "You know Sam's number?"

She nodded and recited it to me, shouting at the top of her lungs to make herself heard amid the prevailing din. I punched the digits as fast as I could while driving left-handed and waited. Norwood answered on the first ring. I filled him in on our situation and gave him a readout of the coordinates on the GPS screen. He instructed me to leave the phone connection open, to triangulate our call, and set course for Druif Bay; Greenwald and Benson would be waiting there, they were in the process of setting up an ambush for the enemy.

"Pat!" Jessica shouted as soon as I put the handset down. "You're bleeding!"

She was right, not only were both my wounds bleeding, my face as well. But who the hell had time to worry about that now?!

"Let's head for Druif!" I told her. "Greenwald and Benson are waiting for us there; don't worry, Carrots, they will take care of holding off the enemy."

"There are only two vehicles left now," she confirmed, "and they have become more cautious."

I tried again to reach Norwood through the radio-transmitter and this time it worked.

"Sam, it's Delta, we're at Manchebo Beach now, heading for Divi. We will be there soon! Over."

"Sounds good, Delta. All set here, just pull off the road as soon as you see us. We'll take it from there. I repeat, pull off the road and lie still, we'll handle it. Do you copy? Over."

"Roger that! Over and out."

I looked back in the rearview mirror, the BMWs continued after us like a pack of hungry wolves that wouldn't give up, but they were maintaining their distance. I slowed down a bit and they sped up their approach.

"Blast away the fuckers, Phi, do it *now*!" I shouted. The wind and the hubbub of nighttime traffic found resonance in the cockpit of the vehicle. Phi prepared herself to carry out the order, but a barrage of 9-millimeter slugs engulfed us like an enraged swarm of deadly wasps. The enemy shots were not a reassuring element, quite the contrary; however, between the bursts of automatic fire, old Tilson's Browning shotgun made itself heard, booming like the cannon fire of a Howitzer.

Eying the action through the rearview mirror, I watched the windshield of the first car explode into multiple fragments, showering us in an avalanche of broken glass and shrapnel. Jessica let out a dreadful howl as another swarm of bullets impacted the rear wheels of our vehicle. I lost control for a critical moment. Phi dropped the shotgun and lay on her side, curled into a ball, clutching her left shoulder and side as her body jumped around the lurching vehicle. She groaned in pain, and I could see blood dripping down her arm.

Having lost control of the rear wheels, the SUV began to slide sideways and went off the road. We hit a tree trunk hard. I bounced my head against the windshield. Stunned by the bump, I told myself that we had done everything possible to accomplish the mission, and now we had come to the end of the road... It was at that moment that Norwood's chopper materialized out of the night as if by magic! The roar of its blades hit me all at once, as the sand on the beach began to fly around us, creating a real pandemonium. For a few moments, our situation was best described as hell on Earth. The big mechanical bird just seemed to hover above us, absorbed in the task of trying to locate us. Then it tilted its nose to the ground, lifted its tail and circled; making the earth tremble with the force of the propellers, it went off to face the enemy.

I'm not sure if those poor bastards died knowing what hit them, but the battle was over in a matter of seconds. The only thing I remember, before losing consciousness, were two terrible streaks of fire (like the breath of a dragon) tracing their way through the night in a trajectory that began in the air and ended on the ground, blasting the pursuing cars off the road.

"Die hard, motherfuckers!" I growled before losing consciousness once and for all. "The party is over!"

After that I knew no more.

*E*pilogue

The outcome of that dramatic episode at Divi Beach could very well be described as bizarre, among other things, because I would not see my partner Phi again for several months. Perhaps that was what affected me most. According to what the Colonel told me some time later, we were flown out of Aruba in the same private chopper of the Royal Sky Flying Group, Ltd. by Agent Norwood, but that had been our original plan.

Marlon Berkowitz briefed me that the FBI men transported us to their camouflaged base in the Netherlands Antilles, where we were put in a private Learjet that flew us back to the Opa Locka Airport in Florida. It was at this point that Jessica and I parted ways. I ended up in Mercy Hospital, near Biscayne Bay, stuck in a room on the sixth floor overlooking the inlet for the next three weeks. My boss came to visit me on the third day of convalescence. The doctors —the Colonel informed me— did a good job patching me up; it was made clear to him by the medics that I wouldn't die from this one. And so it was that I came to find myself bedridden, hooked up to an intravenous feeding unit.

"How are you feeling, Delta?" asked my boss, smiling radiantly, obviously pleased to see me improving. If it were up to him, he'd be sending me out on some other tough assignment by now.

As he approached my bed, I noticed a few streaks of

weariness around his eyes. He was wearing his typical attire, a gray 2-piece business suit from Brook Brothers that somehow made him look like a Wall Street stockbroker; he could've been mistaken for a banker as well, or a respectable member of the Greater Miami Chamber of Commerce. The color gray suited him just fine; after all, what else was Marlon Berkowitz but a "gray eminence" of the Counterintelligence services. Staring at him, no man would have suspected that he was in the presence of one of the most dangerous men in the planet.

"I feel swell, sir," I answered his question, "ready to start a long vacation."

"Tsk, tsk," he joked, clicking his tongue, "you've become an ambitious, dreamy man."

"Good to see you, Colonel. This place is already getting on my nerves. Have they told you how much longer they plan to keep me here?"

"I'm not sure, Delta; maybe another week, or two. Dr. Lewis is not comfortable with the way the shredded ligaments in the elbow are healing. After forty, he says, the tissue recoveries are slower."

"Two weeks!!" I bellowed, unable to restrain myself.

"Calm down; it could drag on if you don't cooperate. And I need you back, ASAP."

I gave a disdainful look at the arm that had been operated on. I could not believe it: two more freaking weeks in this bloody place!

"What about the shot in my hip, am I going to become a cripple?"

"Don't exaggerate, Delta, it's just a flesh wound. Dr. Lewis thinks it will not give you any trouble."

"Dr. Lewis..., yes, sir. Who's the guy?"

The Colonel paid no mind to my claim for he knew as well as I did that Dr. Kenneth Lewis was no stranger to me, but now he was keeping a watchful eye on me as if trying to pick my brain.

"What's eating you up, Delta? Anything you want to ask me?"

I never grasped why he bothered asking; it was obvious. I stared him in the eye and pushed my jaw out.

"If you are worrying about *her*, don't...." he said immediately, "like yourself, she's not going to die from this one. It just happens that after going through the reports and hearing from Sam about the way you went out on a limb over there for her... Well, I will not lie to you, Delta, I'm very concerned about your unexpected reaction and thought it might be best to separate the two of you —at least, for the time being. You've always preferred to work alone, haven't you? Well, I will oblige this time."

He had suddenly become very serious, and I realized that this was not an issue on which I should confront him.

"Perfectly understandable, sir." I said, employing a bit of reverse psychology. "I'm glad you finally realized it. I told you flat out I'm not made for teamwork when *you* insisted on setting me up with her after the clash with Goliath in Operation High Keys*, remember? But you know I always obey your orders, sir. Whatever they may be."

He didn't buy it, mind you —well, neither did I— but it was worth a try anyway.

"Don't try to fool me, Delta," he hissed in that flat, menacing tone of his that had become known among the troops as his "death whisper."

"You should have never stuck out your neck for her in such a foolish way! It is against the rules! That is what Norwood, Greenwald and Benson were there for!"

"Yes, sir. And I am deeply sorry, sir. It was a simple

matter of foolish chivalry, or perhaps solidarity... God knows. In any case, it will not happen again. I promise."

"You were badly wounded and in a deplorable state of mind and you were... Bah, forget it, I didn't come all this way to lecture you."

Just as well, I thought, keeping my fingers crossed and my mouth shut.

Then he surprised me by softening his tone when he asked: "What happened down there between you and Tilson? I must know."

I let out a sigh and looked straight at him before grinning. "Are you going to tell me that you don't, Colonel? I'm sure you heard it all through that little bug you had someone plant in Agent Norwood's cigarette pack. But, if you ask me, what happened to old Al is the same thing that happens to those who do not feel hugely appreciated after so many, many years of faithful uninterrupted service. He got tired of the Quadrille, sir; he got fed up with *you*, and our present government's ambiguous foreign policy...."

"It had nothing to do with *that*!" He replied with his characteristic stubbornness. "There's something else!"

"Oh, yes. There is." I assured him.

"Arnold Feldman *is* behind this, isn't he?" he asked, and his eyes took on a very disturbing emotional intensity.

"He sure is, sir, you know that. Tilson did not mention him by name, but...."

"Tell me in detail what Tilson said, I want to hear it from your lips."

"Al said he had a message for me that is why he did not finish me off when he had the chance. The message came from a character he referred to as Mr. F."

"And what was the message?"

"Well, Tilson said he had been authorized to tell me,

and I will now go on to quote him verbatim, that 'I had antagonized Mr. F in the Florida Keys, then in Colombia and now in Aruba,' and he mentioned that Mr. F suspected that agents Marvin Rose and Mortimer Long had both died by my own doing, or because of me."

"How interesting. Anything else?"

"Yes. I never admitted in his presence to having neutralized Long, but when I tried to reason with him, he forced me to keep quiet, adding that it was not to him that I was accountable for my actions, but to this Mr. F fella. He added that everyone was aware that I was only your puppet, sir... A trained mastiff, was the exact phrase he used."

The Colonel let out a gasp upon hearing this last comment. "Bloody bastards!" He gushed out. "Tell me, what was your response?"

Here things got a bit knotty for me. I was suddenly assaulted by a feeling of insecurity. I did not know whether to chalk it up to my imagination or if it really happened, but the truth is that I felt guilty without knowing why. The Colonel was the spitting image of a reproving prosecutor, probing my motives, questioning my loyalty. His eyes gleamed like live electrical wires as his powerful mind struggled to invade mine. I felt an enormous pressure on the frontal plane of my skull, as if an overwhelming force were focused on drilling into my forehead to probe the folds of my encephalon.

I said, "I asked him if he was not also one of your puppets. I mean, killing enemy agents or foreign mobsters is one thing, but when it comes to getting rid of a man who has belonged to our outfit for as many years as old Al did, well, that doesn't come easily, sir."

"Agreed," said my boss, "that is why I need to know *everything*. Go on, Delta, what else did Tilson say?"

"He gave me the message: lead or silver. One of those

offers you can't refuse. According to him, the Quadrille is about to be annulled, and Mr. F offered me a position among his hordes. Permanent station on the island of Aruba, under Tilson, of course, but away from the main man himself. He also offered a secret account in one of those offshore banks, with a bundle of tax-free money, all laundered by the Parasol, I guess. Mr. F is up to his neck in the pie with the Russian mobsters, sir, or he was planning to steal their laundered money using Tilson and Goriainov."

"*That's* what I'm afraid of," my boss said wrinkling his face into a circumstantial grimace, then he began to take slow steps around the room while nibbling on one knuckle of his right hand, "though not many people on Capitol Hill will believe me. *Who? Arnold Feldman?* They would say. *That 'unimpeachable champion' of American justice stealing from the Russian mob? Unthinkable!* Pretty ironic, isn't it? But Phi's report contains some details that do not emerge in the recount you just gave me. Of course, your points of view become dissimilar when you were ambushed by Tilson's men on the roof of the Royal Hacienda. Norwood says that the shooter you took out was not a clan enforcer, the man turned out to be one of the OCF's operators on Tilson's Caribbean taskforce."

Reminding me of that caused me to frown. Yet another aggression against Mr. F for which I would have to atone....

"Well, Tilson mentioned something about that, but due to my mood at the time, I did not think much of it."

"What you still don't know is that while you were being ambushed by Tilson, Phi ran into two very interesting characters inside the Casino, and I say 'interesting' because even I had no idea that they would show up in Aruba that very night. Of course, now that I think about it, it fits perfectly that they would do so, being the Caribbean umbrella the money-laundering network par excellence for the entire Russian underworld."

He stopped for a second and grinned.

"Just imagine, Delta, if we do what Tilson did, set up permanent surveillance in Aruba, how many important miscreants we could detect, book and eliminate discreetly, once we have them under the radar, eh?"

"Lots of them, naturally."

"There you are!"

"It's a magnificent idea, sir, but why don't you just tell me who the hell Jessica discovered in the Casino the night of the hit that I missed out on. My curiosity is killing me!"

His grin widened at my exasperation.

"It's not so surprising, really," he began, stretching the suspense a little further, "given the nature of the place, it's only logical that they would go there looking to meet the bankers...."

"For God's sake, Colonel! Who were they!"

"Yuri Pavenko," he said widening his smile some more, "old Yuri and his daughter, Nina."

She wasn't his daughter; Jessica had confirmed that while investigating those two, but apparently, she hadn't seen fit to set our fearless leader straight on that one, yet.

Nina Tetriak, alias Nina the Gunslinger —as she was known in the Russian underworld— was many things or maybe *everything* to Yuri Pavenko in those days. She was his concubine; she was his partner in the weapons trafficking business; she was his top enforcer and protégé at the same time; Nina was a complete benefit package for the sneaky Russian mobster. And she was everything to him, *except* his daughter.

"Well," I sighed, "it does make sense, doesn't it? They're looking for a place to launder the profits of their illegal arms sales, that much is obvious. But it could also mean that Pavenko isn't playing fair with us, with CI5 I mean. You told me you made a pact with the man: He collaborates with the Quadrille by disclosing the identities of his most dangerous clients to us and we allow little Nina** to continue breathing without causing her any health problems, right?"

"That's the deal, and I don't think Pavenko intends to break it. It has crossed my mind that maybe he is cooking up something big before bringing us up to speed; but he is doing it at his own pace and convenience. One way or another, if the bastard tries to screw us, we'll find out. For now, I plan to give him the benefit of doubt and some room to maneuver."

His words —and something else I had heard from Tilson— got me thinking. "Who is Jackson Bull, Colonel?" I asked, suddenly changing the subject.

The question took him by surprise. First, he opened his mouth in an energetic gesture, as if to reproach me just for asking, but then he held back, thinking better of it. Finally, Col. Berkowitz let out a sigh.

"I must be losing my mind," he mumbled as he wagged his head from side to side, like someone trying to clear his head. "I've never told you about him before, have I?"

"No, sir, but it seems that you have mentioned him to Jessica. Even old Al knew who he is."

"Tilson probably read it in Jessica's report, which we uploaded into the Shared Files Folder. You never care to go over them anyway unless you are directly ordered to do so. That's why you don't know who this Jack character is."

"True, sir. I hardly ever do that."

"Jackson Bull's name comes linked to others that I will mention after to give you a panoramic view of what, probably, will be the near future of the Quadrille. Perhaps I should say our immediate future, considering the results of this last mission in Aruba. I don't think CI5 will continue to operate much longer, Delta; trust me, Arnold Feldman will see to that."

He paused to fill his lungs, before continuing.

"At the closing of Operation Scorpion Tail***, with the death of Agent Long and the CIA's infiltration of the Cartel del Norte del Valle, the escape of Commander Ahmed with the money I got you for Pavenko prompted an investigation that I put Jessica in charge of. I didn't involve you in it because working with computers is not your cup of tea; you know that. The objective was to find out for sure if the CIA is hot on Pavenko's trail, now that Yuri has become our informant and we are obliged to look after him, but also to find out who this Ahmed fellow really is and what are his purposes, although, according to you, Arteaga introduced him as a CIA asset within a Muslim terrorist cell operating in the Middle East... You do remember, don't you?"

"Yes, sir, he also told us that Commander Ahmed belonged to Osama bin Laden's group."

"That's what that man led the CIA to believe; the reality is otherwise. Ahmed does not work for the Central Intelligence Agency nor Bin Laden. He fooled them all. Commander Ahmed is a guerrilla fighter of Palestinian origin, not a Saudi nor a Yemeni, and he has his own army of militants. What do you think of that, eh?

"The Islamic Sword...."

"That is correct."

Now, that depressed me. In the good old days of the Cold War, we had been a very efficient bunch, small and secretive and sometimes underbudget, true, but *extremely* efficient. And in these present days of an evolving New World Order, there were no steps we took without generating a setback... Or so it seemed. I began to feel very unhappy for not having been able to take out that terrorist commander back in Colombia, as I was ordered to, even though we were still unaware of how dangerous the devious bastard was.

"Do not be overwhelmed, Delta; in part this suits us because fighting Ahmed and his Islamic Sword opens another clandestine battlefront and that is what we are for: the Quadrille, the true soldiers of the underground. Arnold Feldman has pinched his own keister with the door; it's not going to be as easy for him to take us out of circulation, as he thinks, because a new war is coming, Delta, one as big and silent as the one we fought against the KGB and with the potential to become an all-out conflagration at a moment's notice."

"So, Phi figured all this out on her own, without anyone's help? If that's the case, sir, hats off to her; and to you as well, for having the good sense to bring her on board."

He was pleased to hear that from my lips, he gave evidence of it by allowing himself a slight grin of satisfaction.

"I told you that in this new world order Intelligence analysts are needed to keep us on the ball. Nowadays it's mostly about electronics and cybernetics knowing what we need to know through computers before we take decisive action. The world has evolved, Delta. But not all the credit goes to Jessica, mind you, Agent Jack Bull and some MOSSAD operatives collaborated to book Commander Ahmed and his secret little army."

"According to what I heard Tilson say, Jackson Bull works for the NRO —what's that, Colonel?"

"It's the National Reconnaissance Office, the most obscure member of our Intelligence Community. Basically, it is another agency of the DOD that oversees many shady areas. One of its recently assigned responsibilities, I've been told, is going after all major dealers in Weapons of Mass Destruction."

"Hell, that's going to put considerable strain in our relationship with Yuri."

"Yes, I know."

His expression hardened for a second, but then he loosened up and smiled at me with jovial mischief.

"Don't worry, Delta, I'll figure out a way to make this NRO man see things our way. Sam Norwood can help us with Jack. In fact, both make excellent material to integrate the new Quadrille now that we've lost Tilson. Don't you think?"

I did not answer that. I was beginning to feel symptoms of exhaustion and the Colonel noticed it. Too much information for the limited intellect of a simple manhunter such as yours truly.

"Anyway," my boss went on, "I'm glad things ended well for us. After all, Operation Parasol has turned out to be successful and, besides, we purged a heretic from our very own group. You gave him my message, didn't you? I trust you did so before the Triple K group put him out of action?"

"I certainly did, Colonel. He got your message." I said weakly.

"Good. I'll be on my way and leave you to get some rest, then. I can tell you need it. You've earned a vacation without interruption, but not before you're fully recovered, okay?"

"Yes, sir," I said, but what I really wanted to do in those very moments was to ask about Jessica.

He was already at the door when he suddenly seemed

to remember something and turned around.

"Gosh, I almost forgot." He muttered as he slipped a hand into the inside pocket of his jacket. "Here, I brought you a little present, Delta, for remaining loyal."

I couldn't suppress an expression of astonishment when I heard this.

"You showed bravery back in Aruba, son. Tactical errors aside, it was a magnificent job, on both parts; she also excelled..." The Colonel snickered with restrained pride and paused to clear his throat. "I hope it's to your liking; mind you, I'm not in the habit of having this kind of gesture with my subordinates."

Having said that, he winked at me, laid the leather case on my chest, and took off. I opened it with a trembling hand, I must confess. If it was a bomb and it blew up in my face, I deserved it, for being a cretin and sentimental.

He had called me son....

It was a beautiful Rolex wristwatch, the *Submariner* model, specially designed for divers. It had luminous hands, a deep blue dial with a large crown which could resist up to 1000 meters deep. But that wasn't all, there was also a legend in Latin engraved on the back cover, it read *Sua sponte*. Translated into English it means "Of its own free will." In a fast-paced unit such as the 75th Ranger Regiment, this motto honors all the volunteers who, "of their own free will," belong to all three branches: Regular Army, Parachute School, and Ranger Regiment. But, in my case —all modesty aside— I had gone one step further, graduating from Sniper School with the highest decorations... And that was the very first time in my life —the only *one*, for that matter— that, given the nature of my anonymous profession, anyone recognized it. I never received a medal for my valor, for being wounded in combat, or for the merit of the covert actions I carried out for God and country.

Only that expensive, fine-looking, diver's watch.

Talking about objects with sentimental values, this watch was it!

A reluctant tear welled up in one of my eyes, but it was quickly suppressed, and I swallowed dryly, battling strong emotions. The Colonel, who had stopped by the door to watch my reaction, turned around and walked away to give me space, and I dare say I won the battle against sentimentality.

Well, almost.

THE END

*Refer to the second volume in the series, entitled *Red Goliath*. (*Author's Note*)
**Refer to the third volume in the series, entitled *One Deadly Souk*. (*Author's Note*)
***Refer to the third volume in the series, entitled *One Deadly Souk*. (*Author's Note*)

.

ABOUT THE AUTHOR

OSCAR ORTIZ was born in 1959 (Matanzas, Cuba), but he was raised in the United States. From an early age he showed a talent for art and literature and (to the same extent) his dislike of collective sports, business, science, and math. He spent his youth studying commercial art & advertising. Ortiz is the winner of the "Sole Second Prize" in the **2006 ENRIQUE LABRADOR RUIZ INTERNATIONAL STORY-WRITERS AWARD** with his crime story *La culpa fue de Hammett* (Blame it on Hammett) and was selected as a finalist in the **2006 TELEMUNDO WRITERS WORKSHOP** contest. He has worked as a freelance screenwriter for Telemundo Puerto Rico and Cubana de Televisión Studios in Miami. He currently resides with his wife in South Florida.